TOTAL WIPEOUT

HE'S WATCHING...

ANNA-MARIE MORGAN

ALSO BY ANNA-MARIE MORGAN

In the DI Giles Series:

Book 1 - Death Master

Book 2 - You Will Die

Book 3 - Total Wipeout

Book 4 - Deep Cut

Book 5 - The Pusher

Book 6 - Gone

Book 7 - Bone Dancer

Book 8 - Blood Lost

Book 9 - Angel of Death

Book 10 - Death in the Air

Book 11 - Death in the Mist

Book 12 - Death under Hypnosis

Book 13 - Fatal Turn

Book 14 - The Edinburgh Murders

© Anna-marie Morgan. All rights reserved. 2016
Edited: David Burton, Economyedits.
Cover: SelfPubBookCovers. com/Shardel

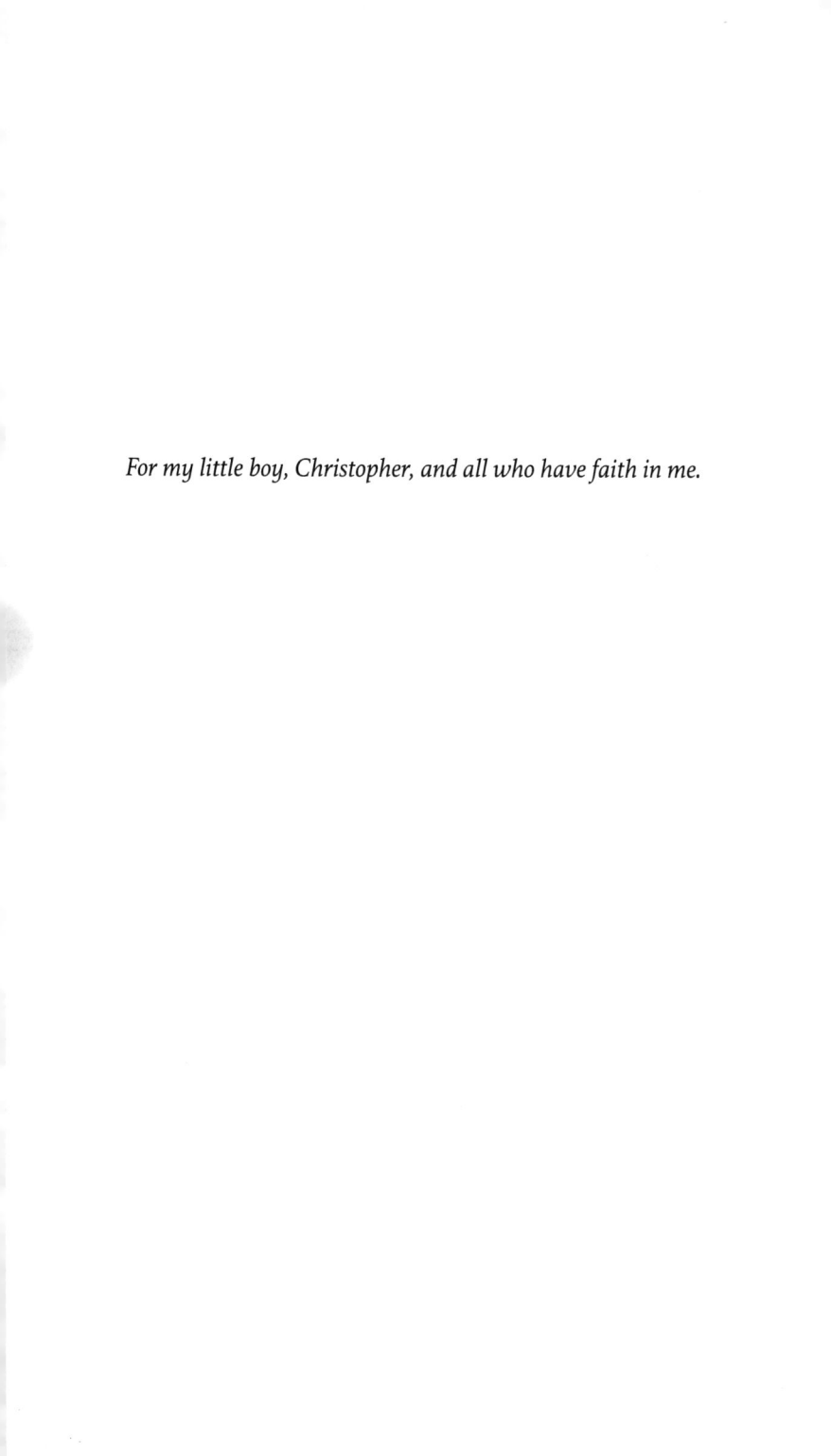

For my little boy, Christopher, and all who have faith in me.

1

"We have a total wipeout."

"Everyone?"

"Even the dog."

Yvonne closed her eyes. Seconds passed. "How many?"

"Five, by the looks of it, ma'am: mum, two daughters, the father, and son. Plus the dog."

"Walk me through it."

DC Callum Jones squeezed past the DI, leading the way to the bedrooms. "No signs of forced entry. We think the father killed the mother first."

Yvonne stared down at the double bed. The woman's face was peaceful, as though asleep, the duvet tucked under her chin. Below this, the cover was a ragged, bloody mess.

She'd been shot at close range with a twelve-bore. Blood spatter had reached three of the four bedroom walls. Tiny spots littered the ceiling. The DI held her breath until she gasped. There were no words.

Stony-faced, DC Jones walked out onto the landing. He turned to check she was following, his sunken eyes a warning of what was to come.

The children's room was further down the long landing. Two small girls, around five or six, shared a double bed. They lay facing each other, their duvet tucked under their chins. Just as with their mother, the cover was a crimson mess.

The little boy, no older than four, lay in his single bed. Eyes closed. Duvet tucked under his chin. Yvonne put a hand to her mouth, as a tear teased its way down her cheek. She stood, a clinically-suited intruder, on a scene peppered my forensic markers, wishing she could click her fingers and turn back time. Go back and save these beautiful children and their mother.

She pulled down her mask and took a deep breath, her legs melting away beneath her. She would have fallen were it not for DC Jones, who put a hand on her elbow.

"The father's in the kitchen." His voice now barely a whisper, he led her back the way they had come.

Mr Davies lay crumpled over the kitchen island, the back of his head missing. The shotgun next to him, covered in blood. Blood and brain matter littered the wall behind. The DI stood in the doorway whilst SOCO worked the room.

"He has spatter on his t-shirt which is not consistent with his injuries." Callum pulled his mask down to address her.

"From his family?"

"More than likely."

"I've asked the team to begin digging into Ben Davies' financial background and contact social services to find out if the family were on their radar."

"How desperate must a man be to destroy himself and his family?"

"If he did..." Yvonne stood very still, lips pursed.

"Well, everything we've seen so far would fit that narrative."

"I know, but it's all a bit snug."

"Ma'am?"

"Oh, I don't know. Something doesn't feel quite right. It's just...I have a nephew and niece of similar ages and I have almost never seen them sleeping so neatly tucked up. Especially Tom, my nephew. He always throws the bedclothes off."

"It was a cool night."

"Yes, yes, I suppose it was." Yvonne shrugged.

Dewi came in from the garden. "Nothing disturbed out there, that we can see. Fingertip search is underway."

"Thanks, Dewi."

As the DI left the house, she turned to face it, still feeling uncomfortable. The eight-bedroom property had a CCTV camera on each front corner. A smaller camera monitored the front porch. The double gates behind her had been closed and padlocked, presumably by Mr Davies. They'd had to use bolt cutters to gain access.

As she looked back at the peaceful view towards Knighton, in the Welsh marches, the DI vaguely recalled the bones of a family wipeout case that had occurred near Shrewsbury. The West Mercia force had dealt with it a few months back. That case had involved a mum, dad, children and family dog. She'd read about it in the local press. She resolved to phone the detectives who'd worked the case.

∼

THAT EVENING, eating a late dinner, Yvonne could see the faces of the Davies children and their mother. Her hunger evaporated. Standing there, in that blood-soaked room, she'd had an overwhelming urge to scoop up those little ones and hold them forever. Kiss those innocent cheeks, which still held their babyhood chubbiness. She thought of her nephew and niece, whom she hadn't seen in six months. She would give her sister Kim a call. Spend the bank holiday with them. Life was too short.

The sun, bedding itself behind the house, coloured the sky a rich orange. A crimson glow settled on the fields. The DI took a large hot chocolate outside, to sit and experience the dusk. Her taut knuckles shone white, as she pondered the dead children. She was still gripping the mug long after its contents were gone, and the last melodic notes of the evening had been uttered by the birds. The night chill had already sent those choristers scuttling to their nests.

Once it was fully dark, she shook off the stiffness penetrating her bones and went back inside, taking the stairs to bed.

2

"Dewi, can you get me the name of the DS who dealt with the family wipeout in Maesbury?"

"Ma'am?"

"I just need to tie up some loose ends."

"Will do."

Yvonne had the Davies family file on her desk, still unable to put it away, even though the early forensic and pathologist's reports leaned towards the culpability of the father. Open-and-shut-case was now the official position.

Tests on the father's t-shirt had shown it to have blood spatter and DNA from every one of his family members. This suggested he'd been present during the murder of each of them. And yet, doubt still curled its invasive tendrils around her.

Her phone pinged in her bag. She fumbled for it. Kim. She felt relief at the reply to her message. She'd texted her sister an hour ago, and Kim was usually faster at replying. Her sister confirmed that Yvonne could join them for the bank holiday weekend. The DI smiled, relishing the thought of seeing her family again.

. . .

She dialled the extension for DS McAllister in the West Mercia force, self-doubt increasing with every ring. The DI was about to give up, when a baritone voice came on the other end. "DS McAllister."

Yvonne cleared her throat. "Hello. DI Giles, Dyfed-Powys

Police. Look, I'm sorry to bother you, DS McAllister, but I wondered if I might ask you a few questions about a family homicide you dealt with a few months back?"

"The Bennetts?"

"Yes, the Bennetts, I believe Mr Bennett killed his family and then himself."

"That's right, a total wipeout. One of the most devastating cases I've dealt with in recent years."

"Did you, at any point, have doubts regarding the culpability of the father?"

"Err...no. Not really,Mr Bennett had huge debts, most of which had been accrued in the six months before he died. He'd self-referred to his GP for depression. All the evidence pointed in one direction. Why do you ask?"

"We've had a similar case. It's early days, so we don't now yet if it's debt-related. We're still investigating motive, but initial forensics are pointing towards the father."

"You're having doubts..."

"I have some niggling questions in my head. I wanted to ask you about the mother and daughter in your case."

"Go on..."

"How were they found? Were they in bed?"

"Yes, all tucked up."

"All tucked up? Were the bedclothes tucked under their chin?"

"Yes, they were. We interpreted that as the dad wanting to care for them, even after he'd killed them. Like he hadn't really wanted to kill them. Like he'd seen it as a necessary evil."

"Do you have the crime scene photographs?"

"Would you like to see the file?"

"Could I?"

"I'll dig the file out and get a copy sent over to you, if it helps."

"It may. I can't thank you enough. Our family was neatly tucked up, too."

As she put the phone down, Yvonne considered approaching Llewellyn, but decided against it. She'd wait to see what Dewi came up with, regarding Mr Davies' finances, and arm herself with the Bennett family crime scene photographs. This was the first family wipeout she'd dealt with. She didn't have a huge amount of experience to draw on, but murder-suicide was generally more chaotic than this.

DEWI HANDED her a pile of papers. "Ben Davies' financial records from his bank and accountant, ma'am."

"Thanks, Dewi." Yvonne examined them, frown lines developing on her forehead. "Half a million in debt? Looks like he was in credit until around six months prior to his death." The frown lines deepened as she recalled her conversation with DS McAllister.

"What are you thinking?" Dewi narrowed his eyes.

"I just had a conversation with West Mercia about their family wipeout case, the Bennetts. Mr Bennett went into debt six months prior to his death."

"Interesting coincidence, ma'am."

"Yes, and I know it's most likely to be just a coincidence, but I want to dig a little deeper: look at the background to this debt in more depth - compare it with the our case. They're sending me the file. I'll read through it all at home. I've got nothing better to do." She gave Dewi a wry smile.

Dewi nodded, though his eyes suggested he believed she was wasting her energy.

3

The view from the castle was spectacular on such a cloudless, clear-view day. He could see for miles across multi-coloured fields and woods. He inhaled the summer-scented air, like he was about to sample a glass of fine wine, and wandered over to where he had the farthest view. He gazed in the general direction of the Ball family residence and took a long swig from his coke can. He held the can to his temple, the ice-cold sheen of water, cooling him down.

He thought of Mrs Ball, putting out family washing on such a day. Reaching up, body taut under her expensive clothes. Sweating in the heat. He felt a stirring in his loin and scratched himself, tossing the can over the wall. It was too public here. He needed somewhere more secluded.

He found the hedge line and followed it until he was sure he was far enough, and hidden away enough, to relieve himself with his hand. Feeling calmer, he pulled up his zipper and glanced around. He could hear the voices of an approaching family but couldn't see the people. Good. That meant they couldn't see him. He hastily began the return walk, around the castle, and descending the hill into the tiny town of Montgomery.

Thirsty, he chose a cafe in the main square below the castle, aptly named 'Castle Kitchen.' It had an aged feel, having a bay window at the front, filled with a variety of tempting cheeses, breads and other local delicacies. Inside was small but welcoming. There was even an open fire, clearly not needed at the moment.

The petite waitress came to meet him. "Hello. What can I get you?"

He examined her: her hair in a neat pony-tail; a cool, white blouse open at the neck, but demurely so. If he'd been honest, she would most probably have telephoned the police. "Have you got beef?"

"We do have beef, sir, from a local farm."

"In that case, I'll have a beef sandwich, with English mustard. Lots of English mustard. Also, a pot of Darjeeling...if you have it."

As he watched her scurry off to fulfil his order, he opened another button on his shirt. It was almost too hot, and he felt it more now he was inside, an uncomfortable moist patch developing on the small of his back. He leaned back in his chair, appreciating the fact that, at the moment, he was the only customer.

She was back, looking quite calm. He examined his sandwich as she watched, peeling up the edge of the bread until he could see a large part of the beef underneath. "I did say lots of mustard."

He thought he caught a quickly-smothered, withering look. If he had, there was no sign of it now as she gave a relaxed smile, before turning on her heel towards the food-prep area.

"Are you here for the day?" she asked, in a distracted fashion.

He could hear the knife in the mustard pot. "I've just been for a walk around the castle. It was very...*satisfying.*" He smiled at his own innuendo.

The sandwich was back. "It's certainly lovely this time of year." If she'd caught his meaning, she didn't show it.

"The Darjeeling?"

"Oh yes, I'm sorry. I'll go get it."

"Thank you."

"Where are you from?" She came through with his tea tray.

"The big smoke."

"Are you here on holiday?"

"Yes." She was asking a lot of questions. A part of him liked that.

"What do you do?"

"Money. I do money. I'd ask you what you do, *but...*" His words dripped intentional contempt.

She looked directly at him. He'd achieved his goal. Her eyes were an inferno. He could feel them, like daggers swiping at him, aiming to cut him down a size. Far bigger fish than her had tried that and failed. She needed sorting out and he was just the man to do it.

"Enjoy your lunch." She was gone.

He was once more alone in the small room, albeit short-lived. The family he had heard up at the castle entered the cafe. He could tell it was them because of the father's deep voice and the shrill, whiny voice of the child, telling his dad exactly what he did and didn't want. He resented their presence.

The smile the waitress furnished on them was far wider than the one she'd given him. She gazed indulgently at the child, and they were all 'please' and 'thank you' and 'sorry to trouble you'.

He pushed back his chair with a loud scrape and palmed the rest of his sandwich. Downing the dregs of his Darjeeling, he left them all behind.

4

The drive to Witney had taken over three hours, avoiding the motorway. Yvonne pulled into the Madley Park residential area, on her way to her sister's house: a three-bedroomed semi with big sky.

As she walked up the garden path, she could feel the tension leaving her body. Kim came out to greet her, a glass of ice-cold juice at the ready. Yvonne exchanged cheek-kisses and gratefully accepted the drink, jumping when her five-year-old nephew Tom rammed his big and colourful, plastic truck into the back of her calves.

"It's good to see you, sis." Kim put an arm around her.

Yvonne smiled broadly. "I've missed you. *And* you," she said to the giggling Tom. He stood looking up at her, all sandy-haired and freckle-faced, chocolate round his mouth.

"Where's Sally?" The DI asked, looking for her six-year-old niece.

Kim looked all about her. "Still in the back garden, I think. We've just fired up the barbecue."

"I thought I could smell something." Yvonne rubbed her

tummy, bending down and scooping Tom up into her arms. "Mmmmm. I think I could eat a horse."

Tom giggled again, and threw his arms around his aunty's neck. "We've got sausages and chicken and... and..." He struggled to remember what else his mum had told him. "Potato salad!" He remembered with a self-satisfied flourish.

"That sounds absolutely to-die-for." Yvonne gave him a broad smile, hugging him tightly and kissing the end of his nose. "Come on, let's find your sister."

Sally watched the barbecue coals, as the flames began to die back. When she saw her aunt enter the garden, still with Tom in her arms, she ran over to her - almost falling in her excitement. She curled her arms around Yvonne's thighs. "Aunty Yvonne!"

"Well, hello, little lady, it's good to see you, too. What have you got for me over here?"

"We've just lit the barbecue and mummy's going to clean it with a special brush." Sally pushed back tiny, blonde curls from her face and stared back into the barbecue.

"Not too close, Sally." Kim had her hands full with two large trays of food.

"Here, let me help." Yvonne popped little Tom back on his feet and took one of the trays, from her sister. In this moment, she felt deeply happy. It was good to be back with her family with all its noisy chaos. Such a contrast to her own life back in Wales.

"How's the house?" Kim asked, scrubbing the barbecue's iron grid with a wire brush.

"It's coming along. Still quite a bit of work to do and not enough time, you know."

Kim nodded. "You work too hard."

"Says you: single-mum extraordinaire. I don't know how you do it."

"Well, I only work part-time."

"No such thing as part-time in your life." Yvonne grinned, giving a wink in the little ones' direction.

"You have a point there." Kim laughed.

"I missed you."

"We missed you, too. Six months is too long. My kids adore you."

"I've worked a couple of difficult cases but that's no excuse. I won't leave it so long next time."

THE REST of the afternoon passed in a flurry of food and activity, until bulging, dark clouds filled the late-afternoon sky and the first drops of rain fell. They ran into the house whooping and screaming in a race to get out of the rain. Sally won, followed by Tom, then Kim and Yvonne, pretending to be out of puff and well-beaten.

Yvonne helped Tom build a rocket out of Lego, and Sally change her dolly's nappy. At this point, Kim announced it was time for the children's baths. They'd had a good afternoon and were thoroughly grubby.

"Can Aunty Yvonne put us to bed?" Sally asked, pulling on her mum's sleeve.

"I think you'd better ask Aunty Yvonne..."

"Can you? Please. Please?"

Yvonne pretended to consider.

"Pleeeeeeeeease?" Sally and Tom begged in unison.

Yvonne laughed at the two expectant faces. "Oh, go on then."

"Yay!"

. . .

HALF-AN-HOUR LATER, she was carrying a child on each hip up the stairs to their bedroom, whilst promising to read them two bedtime stories. Her back complaining, she wondered how her sister managed to carry them like this many times a day.

She kissed the tops of each of their heads, and took in the freshly washed, sweet smell of their hair. Her heart ached. It ached for the children she herself had wanted with David. The children she was destined never to have. She hugged them tight, before setting each one down on their beds and tucking them in.

One and a half stories later, their eyes had closed. Tom had already pushed the bedclothes off his chest, his favourite cuddle-blanket curled in his arms. Sally held her doll, which she'd just kissed goodnight. They looked so peaceful.

Unbidden, came that dreadful scene she had witnessed in that home, in Knighton. Those three little ones blown away. Their faces not unlike the two peaceful ones before her now. It struck her then. She didn't recall any of them cuddling anything, not even a favourite toy or a blanket. Why not?

SHE REJOINED a tired-looking Kim in the lounge. They each let out a large yawn.

"Glass of white?" Her sister handed her a glass which she gratefully accepted.

"I don't know how you do it," she chuckled. "Those two are like whirlwinds."

"You'd make a great mum, Yvonne."

Yvonne gave a wistful sigh. "Maybe one day."

"Have you spoken to mum recently?"

"Not for a while... You?"

"She misses you, you know."

"We've had this discussion. I speak to her now and again. Anyway, it's more important that you keep in touch with her, for the children. They need a grandma."

Kim nodded. "They Skype with her regularly, though the time difference makes it tricky."

"Adelaide is a world away."

"It'll be the tenth anniversary of dad's..." Kim's voice faded.

"Next month. Yeah, I know."

"It's why she ran away, you know."

"With him. I'd have had more respect if she'd gone alone."

"Affairs happen, sis. They couldn't have known that dad would..." Kim grimaced.

"Take his own life? You can say it, Kim, it won't kill him again." Yvonne saw her sister's sadness and relented. "I'm sorry. I miss him, too. And I miss mom. I just can't help the strong feelings I have towards that *man*. At least dad didn't try to take her with him."

Kim looked at her sister, open-mouthed, eyes wide.

"I didn't mean it like that. It's just a case I'm working on. The dad allegedly took everyone in the family with him. It happens sometimes."

Kim's face relaxed. "I thought you meant you thought him capable."

"No, no, definitely not. In fact, I have a feeling neither did the father-in-question, but I'm having a hard time convincing anyone I work with of that."

"Hey, forget work," Kim chided. "You're here with *us* now. Cheers."

Yvonne smiled ruefully. "Cheers."

. . .

The file from DS McAllister lay on her desk on Tuesday morning. Yvonne immediately sat down with it, flipping through in order to start with the crime-scene photographs. "Dewi?"

"Yes, ma'am."

"Can you get me the file for the Davies family."

"Will do. What are you up to?"

"Comparing it to the one from West Mercia."

"Okay, ma'am." Dewi pulled a face.

"Now?"

Dewi grinned. "Right-oh."

Mrs Bennett could have been Mrs Davies. Different hair colour but the same tucked-up peacefulness of the crime scene. Yvonne drew in a deep breath, her heart beating just a little faster. The teenage daughter – similar. The little boy of five – same again. Even down to the direction their heads were facing: towards the left, all peaceful. Bloody duvets tucked up tight under their chins. The Bennett father had been found in the garden. Shot through the mouth, the back of his head blown away. Blood-spatter from his family all over his t-shirt.

She continued to turn the pages. Finances. He'd lost heavily. Gone from credit to debit six months before, and owed creditors more than a million. His clothing business had gone into administration. The bank had wanted his home, thought to be worth just shy of a million. His Porsche had been repossessed. Motive enough, perhaps, to take his own life. But to take his family's lives? Perhaps, but those crime scenes, and the similarity to her own crime scenes, left her even more doubtful.

She ran her thoughts past Dewi, who'd brought her coffee and a Chelsea bun from Evans' cafe.

"I get what you're saying," Dewi said with his mouth full. "It's just that it wouldn't be beyond the realms of possibility that two dads would tuck their loved ones up after killing them. Like a last act kindness. Their way of saying sorry."

"Okay, but just look at the children."

"I'm looking..."

"Not one of them over six years old."

"Uhuh..." He shook his head blankly.

"Well, not one of them is holding a teddy, cuddle-blanket or favourite toy. You've had children. Don't you find that unusual? My nephew and niece always sleep cuddled up to something."

Dewi grabbed the file and peered a little more closely at the photos. "Well, you're right about that." He leaned back. "I still don't think that'll be enough to convince anyone to look more deeply, given the state of both the fathers' finances."

"You looked at the Bennett file, then." Yvonne gave her DS a raised-eyebrow look.

"I did. And I can tell you I have some sympathy for your position."

"There's something else."

"Go on."

"Looking at the floor plans, there's some distance between the children's rooms and the parents room. In the Bennett case, there was even the separation of a floor."

"So..." Dewi screwed up his face.

"So, the children could have been killed without waking the parents up."

"I still don't think that's enough to persuade anyone to keep the case open."

Yvonne shrugged. "Well, I'm going to try Llewellyn, anyway. He can but turn me down and, in the meantime, Dewi, I want you to dig deep into the backgrounds of these two men. Find out *why* the sudden downturns in fortune. I want to know who their business associates were."

Dewi nodded, grinning. He could see the fight in her, and admired her courage to take on their superiors.

HE ENJOYED DUSK. One of his favourite times. The encroaching darkness, whilst making most of humanity feel less safe, helped him feel powerful. To see and not be seen. That's what it was about. They liked their glass, modern families. Flaunting their lives. Allowing the likes of him better access. Little did they know.

He took a swig from his coke can, then ran its coldness over his forehead. From up among the trees, he could see the house clearly. The lights were on. He took out his binoculars, searching each window for *her*.

When he found her, she was kissing one of her children goodnight, cuddling him tight and smelling his hair. Smiling indulgently, in that proud mother way. After she'd tucked him in, she came to the window. Looking out on the night. She wouldn't see him from where she was.

Deborah Ball was dressed ready for bed. A flimsy, pyjama-shorts all-in-one. Silk by the look of it. He imagined running his hands over her, whilst she wore it. Not that he would get to do this for real. He didn't touch them before dispatching them. No, the pleasure was in the build-up. The creation of the perfect conditions for his finale: the final possession of their lives.

He changed windows when Mrs Ball closed the blinds, blocking his view. Tony Ball was in his study, looking dishevelled, pouring over papers he'd probably poured over before: desperate for them to tell him his ship wasn't sinking, and sinking fast. Head in his hands, shoulders hunched. The look of defeat.

With a jolt, Tony Ball sat upright, the expression on his face morphed to a smile. Deborah had joined him. He could see Tony closing his folder and pushing his chair back, for his wife to sit on his knee, and the watcher felt the hot knife of jealousy in his gut, twisting and sending tingles up his sides and down his thighs.

He put the caps on his binoculars, stowing them in his canvas bag. He'd wait until it was completely dark, before heading back down the lane.

5

Yvonne tentatively rapped on DCI Llewellyn's door.

"Come in." His voice cracked, sounded hoarse.

"Cold, sir?" she asked, as she entered.

"Had the darn thing for a couple of days now. What can I do for you?" He blew his nose and put his handkerchief back in his pocket.

"I want to talk to you about the Davies case, sir."

"The family homicide case?"

"Yes."

"Go ahead. I was going to speak to you about it sometime today."

"I want permission to carry on investigating for a while."

"Errr...that's what I want to speak to you about."

"You're not telling me you're shutting it down?"

"Well, everything we have points directly at the father. We have forensics from his clothing and from the gun. His finances were a mess and he'd self-referred to his GP for depression. It's as near to an open-and-shut case as we ever get, and the superintendent is cock-a-hoop that we don't need to spend any further time or resources on it. The budget's under the cosh by all accounts." The DI was biting her lip. "Yvonne? You're going to tell me you have other thoughts..."

"It's all a bit snug."

"And that's your evidence for having the case stay open, is it?"

"It's a little more than that, sir. I've been comparing case files with a similar family murder from West Mercia, happened four months ago. The death scenes – the positioning of the bodies – they're pretty near identical. The mothers and children were all tucked up, covers under their chins. Their heads were even facing to the same side. What are the chances of that?"

"They were killed in their beds, Yvonne."

"Both fathers had been financially sound until six months prior to their deaths. Six months in both cases. That's a hell of a coincidence."

"Coincidences happen."

"Maybe they do, but, when it comes to multiple murder, I don't believe in them."

"Desperate men do desperate things, Yvonne."

Yvonne thought of her father and her eyes glazed over. "I know. I know they do."

"Yvonne?"

The DI jumped. "I just don't think they did in these cases." She said the words but, for the first time, had some doubt about them. Her father had taken the ultimate step. He'd taken them all by surprise. He just hadn't taken them all with him.

"Look," Llewellyn sighed. "I'd love to lend you my support. I really value your intuition. But I'll need more than you're giving me to take to the super."

Yvonne nodded, feeling defeated, tired or both. "Okay. If I get anything else, I'll come back."

"I'll take another look, if it's by the end of the week, but I don't want you wasting time on this case once it's officially closed."?

"Understood."

6

She gave a nod to the two constables at the gate, flashing her ID. She knew they'd write her name down, noting that she'd visited the scene again, but she didn't care. And anyway, the case wasn't officially closed, yet. She still had until the end of the week to find something. After that, the crime scene would be cleared; the house sold by the bank; a new family moved in, and the Davies family forgotten by the world at large.

Yvonne pushed aside the blue and white tape and entered through the front door. The house had already begun to take on that distinctive smell of abandonment: the onset of damp, with its distinctive mould aroma; fading food and activity smells lingering in household fabrics; and wood, expanding where rain had penetrated.

It was a beautiful residence with a modern interior. Lots of light, high ceilings and mezzanine floors. No curtains. For the first time, she wondered if a killer had watched the family. Could they have been stalked? There were blinds on some of the windows, but, at least downstairs, it looked like they hadn't been used for some time, judging by the dust patterns. A house like this wasn't designed for window coverings, but had that made its occupants easy prey for the eyes of a predator? Was it someone who knew the family well? The village of Knighton was small and tucked away amongst the Powys hills. She didn't imagine this to be an obvious haunt for a stranger.

Yvonne climbed the stairs the glass-and-metal stairs to the bedrooms. She entered the children's room. It was light and spacious. Vertical blinds hung on the windows, and it was clear to the DI they'd been in regular use. With so many bedrooms in the house, she guessed that the three children were roomed together to prevent their fear of the dark.

A lump developed in her throat and her stomach muscles clenched, as she looked down upon the beds. The children were gone, but Yvonne could so easily recall them, they might still be lying there. The blood and biological spatter was as it had been when forensics left. She took her own photographs with her mobile.

Around the room, on floating shelves, were books and teddy bears, dolls and puzzles. On the floor were scattered building bricks, Lego and a push trolley. A part-built Lego robot sat looking sorry for itself, and next to the little girls' bed lay a story book, perhaps containing the last story they had heard. Not for the first time, the DI felt hot tears wending their way down her face, and longed to scoop up those little ones and make everything all right.

On a high shelf, she found two small blankets. Too small to be bed coverings. She held them to her nose and recognised the smell from her nephew and niece's cuddle-blankets. These blankets had been dragged everywhere.

A small bear was sat within them both, and his smell was also reminiscent of a cuddle-toy. He looked well-worn. Why were they on a shelf and not tucked up with the children? Why had nothing cuddly been found in the children's beds? Had a killer removed them? If he had, he had taken them from the sleeping children prior to killing them, as they contained no blood. Was this the act of a psychopath? A loving father, who would tuck his children up in bed after killing them, would surely not remove their favourite things before doing so. Those two actions were diametrically opposed. If they had gone to sleep with cuddle toys, someone removed them. That someone was *not* a loving parent.

She left the children's room, heading for the parents' bedroom. If she shut out the bloody mess that was now the bed and the walls, this was a large and tranquil space. Designed to be restful, with fabrics of whites, creams and greys – in contrast to the bright colours in the children's room. She took more photographs.

Again, it was easy to recall Mrs Davies' body, the bloody cover tucked under her chin. The blood and brain spatter remained. Killed in her sleep. Was she killed first? Or were the children killed first? There was enough distance between the rooms that it was possible she wouldn't have woken at the noise, if they were.

On a whim, the DI checked the bathroom cabinet. She took out the few packets of pills. Two of them had prescription labels, both of which were for Mrs Davies. One of them she recognised as sleeping pills. She'd know from the pharmacology report, as soon as it was in, whether Mrs Davies had taken any the night she died.

She took the stairs to the ground floor and walked the several hundred yards to the kitchen-diner, at the back of the house. Ben Davies had been slumped on the island. Nothing else in the room was disturbed. Blood had spattered on top of the island, on the floor behind him, and on the wall at the back. No footprints had been found in the blood.

If she didn't conform to the official school of thought, she could start with a scenario of Ben being killed first. In fact, she didn't see how a killer could destroy the man's family without him intervening, even at the risk of his own life. No, if she was right, Ben Davies was killed first. That meant the killer somehow got blood from the victims onto the father's shirt *after* he was already dead.

She recalled the positioning of the body and knelt down, to examine underneath the oak breakfast bar. She took out a pocket torch. There was nothing obvious, perhaps a slight discolouration. She took out latex gloves and the swab kit from her bag, and ran a cotton bud along the length of the underside of the oak ledge, where the dad had been positioned, placing it in the sterilin. She just about had time to get this off to forensics before the dreaded deadline.

The final room she wanted to access was Mr Davies' study. This was where he would have stressed about his financial situation, especially if hiding it from his family. This was also where he would have made any plans.

It was another spacious and light room. Sparse furnishings, with a large wood and steel desk, which appeared custom-made for the space. A wall of books towered over one side, the top shelves of which were accessed via a slide-along ladder.

On his desk, was scattered the remains of Mr Davies' paperwork, the rest having been taken by investigators. There was a brochure for canal-barge holidays. Ironically, these were full of smiling families, enjoying summer sunshine. This might have been one of the last things her browsed before his death. Or perhaps he'd had the pamphlet for ages and had dismissed the holiday idea.

The view through his main window was of the well-groomed garden, surrounded by trees and shrubs. A place where a killer might lurk, unseen.

THE NEAREST NEIGHBOURS, also good friends of the Davies family, lived several hundred metres away, in another large house. Yvonne banged hard on the knocker.

"Mrs Swanson?" Yvonne asked, when a forty-something lady with dark, wavy hair, opened the door, looking ashen but otherwise well.

"Yes, I'm Mrs Swanson. What's happened?" she asked when the DI gave her name, flashing her ID.

"I understand you knew the Davies family..."

"I did. They were my friends. Are you here because of what happened?"

"I've come to ask you how well you knew them, and to find out more about them, if that's okay with you."

Mrs Swanson ushered her in and closed the door, leading her into a comfortable lounge. "Please take a seat. Can I get you a cup of tea?"

"No thank you, Mrs Swanson."

"We'd known them for about five years. Ben was an old business associate of Ted's...that's my husband. It was our suggestion that they see that house, when they were looking to buy. Sheila Davies became my best friend. Our children played together."

Yvonne could see the pain in Mrs Swanson's eyes. "Did your children ever have sleepovers?"

"Frequently."

"And the Davies children, did they sleep at yours?"

"Yes..." Mrs Swanson looked puzzled at the question.

"Would you have noticed if the children had cuddle-blankets or cuddle-toys?"

"Cwtches? Yes, they did. Never came here without them. Little Stephen would cry and cry if he'd forgotten his, and Ted would run over and get it. Our whole family is absolutely devastated."

"Mrs Swanson -"

"Kelly."

"Kelly, I'm really sorry for your loss. It must have been a real shock."

"Never saw it coming. I've talked to Ted about it over and over. Neither of us had any inkling. They were a close family. We talked about whether they might have made a pact."

A pact. Yvonne hadn't thought of that. "And what were your thoughts about that?"

"Not possible. Even if Sheila and Ben had decided to end it all, they would not have taken their children with them."

"How sure are you about that? You had only known them for five years."

"Ted had known them longer. For the five years I had known them, we were really close. We holidayed together regularly and had family barbecues. We talked about just about everything and always run stuff past each other, if we were thinking of doing anything unusual."

"And you're sure they wouldn't have killed their own children?"

"I'm positive."

"Did they ever talk to you about money troubles?" Yvonne asked, scribbling madly.

"Ben discussed financial concerns with Ted. They'd leave us and go off and talk about stuff. Sheila didn't mention it to me... Not once. Ben was trying to shield his wife and children as much as possible. But Ted would talk to me when we went to bed at night. He was really worried about Ben's health, him shouldering all that worry by himself. I guess it was much harder for him than even we realised."

"Did Sheila take sleeping tablets?"

"Only when she needed to."

"Was anything worrying her? Why did she take them?"

"She had periods of insomnia. I think it was investigated medically and no reason was found. Like I said, she took them when she needed to."

"How much did Ted know about Ben's financial or business worries?"

"I don't know for sure, but I'd hazard a guess it was pretty much everything. They were that close."

"Did the family have any other concerns besides financial ones?"

"None that I'm aware of. They were happy. The children were happy."

"I saw a brochure for canal holidays on Ben's desk. Were they planning a break?"

"Ted said that Ben had been seriously thinking about buying a barge and making a major life change: the whole family living on a barge. Apparently, he brightened up whenever he talked about it. The idea, this year, was that we all go on a barge holiday together, to give it a try. See how feasible it might be."

"That doesn't sound to me like someone who intended to kill himself and his family."

"No. Exactly. I think if he did decide to end it all, it was a spur of the moment thing. I cannot believe that he planned it."

"You said he brightened up when he talked about the barge. I understand he was being treated for depression."

"He was. He'd been under the doctor for a couple of months. Ted encouraged him to go when he was feeling down."

"As far as you know, Kelly, would they have lost everything as a result of the difficulties Ben was in?"

"Pretty much. The barge was his dream way out."

Yvonne closed her notebook and placed it in her bag, aware that she had a swab sample in there. She needed to get it to the lab. "Thank you for your help today, Kelly. It can't have been easy for you to talk about this. I've filled in quite a few gaps with your information."

"It can't have been easy for you, either."

"I'm sorry?"

"Seeing what you saw. I'm sure you've seen things I hope I'll never see."

Yvonne thought of the children and nodded. "It doesn't get any easier."

7

When Yvonne got back to the station, she handed him her package to Dewi. "Can you get that to the lab, ASAP? Let them know that the DNA may not yield much. Probably too degraded, but I think that's blood, and I'd like to know if it is or not. I almost certainly couldn't use it in evidence but the results will tell me if I'm thinking in the right ball-park. I have a theory." She pulled a face.

"Where have you *been* all afternoon? Have you been back to the house?"

"Why? Did you miss me? And yes, I went back to the house."

"Does Llewellyn know?"

"Does he have to know?"

Dewi grinned. He was getting used to his DI answering a question with a question. "No, I guess not."

"Great. Get that sample off for me, please, whilst you're still allowed to." Yvonne grinned back.

When Dewi returned, he had some paperwork for her. "This is why I was looking for you this afternoon, ma'am."

"Good work, Dewi." Yvonne gratefully accepted the paperwork, spotting at a glance that this was the financial information she'd asked for on Ben Davies.

"Ah, Yvonne." DCI Llewellyn came around the corner, a stern look on his face.

"Sir?" Yvonne straightened up.

He handed her some papers. "I'm putting you on a rape case. Victim was attacked last night in Welshpool." He rubbed his forehead. "Unusual case. Very much looks like it was a carefully planned attack."

"But, sir, what about the Davies family deaths? I..."

"What about them? We've had this conversation, Yvonne. There's nothing to solve. The case is officially closing."

"But - "

"Someone was raped last night. I want you and your team to find the rapist."

"Very well, sir."

YVONNE AND DEWI joined uniform officers who were comforting the girl. Dewi stayed outside of the interview room whilst Yvonne, a victim liaison officer, and the WPC who'd been with the girl throughout, went inside.

The girl was petite, dark-haired and aged nineteen years. She sat in a paper suit, visibly shaken, bearing the scars of her ordeal everywhere: bruises, grazes and red welts. Yvonne immediately felt guilty about her earlier irritation towards working this case.

"Good afternoon, errr..." Yvonne looked down at her paperwork. "Ms Pugh. Can I call you Tina?"

"Yes." The girl nodded, and wiped her eye with the back

of her hand, having long since stopped worrying about streaking her mascara.

"I'm Detective Inspector Yvonne Giles. I work with CID. I'm going to find who did this to you, okay?"

The girl nodded, her eyes focused on the table.

"Can I get you anything? A cup of tea? Food?"

The girl shook her head.

"Tell me what happened."

"I worked my usual shift and -"

"I'm sorry, where were you working?"

The girl looked up and her brilliant-blue eyes met those of the DI for the first time. "I work at The Castle Cafe in Montgomery."

"Go on."

"I finished my shift and drove home to Welshpool. I'd organised to meet my friends at six-thirty pm, to go out in the town. We'd begun with drinks in The Angel, and intended ending up in The Lounge nightclub. The Lounge doesn't open until eleven pm so we were a bit tipsy by that time."

"Define tipsy."

"Well, I'd paced myself. I'd had a couple of soft drinks, here and there, just to make sure I stayed sensible. I hate not being able to remember anything."

"I see. What happened then?"

"My friends were a little more drunk than I was and wanted to rush their drinks before the club. I needed the toilet and I didn't want to rush mine. In the end, I told them to go and I'd catch up. We didn't have that far to go."

"So you were walking alone when you left The Angel?"

"Yes, I walked quickly, but my friends had disappeared into the club."

"What happened then?"

"I was grabbed from behind and pulled into the alley. He had gloves, dark clothing and a mask on. He smelled of soap. He raped me." The girl began crying again and Yvonne reached over and placed her hand on the girl's hands, looking over at the WPC.

"Do we have swabs?"

The WPC shook her head. "We think he wore a condom, ma'am. No trace of semen, but plenty of evidence of forced penetration. Forensics have the girl's clothes. We're hoping there'll be hairs or fibres on those."

"And CCTV?"

"The only CCTV pictures are useless. Too dark and grainy to identify someone so heavily disguised."

"Did he say anything to you?" Yvonne's attention was back on the girl.

"No, nothing."

"We'll do our very best to find him, Tina. I can promise that."

The girl gave a sob and was comforted by the support officer.

8

Late evening saw Yvonne pouring over Ben Davies' financial information. Next to her was the file DS McAllister had sent from West Mercia on the Bennett family from Maesbury March.

She didn't know a huge amount about hedge funds but she'd need to apprise herself, and quickly. It appeared both Davies and Bennett had been accredited hedge fund investors, and had ploughed a lot of money into short-term investments, via a London hedge fund management firm.

They had both liquidated longer-term investments prior to doing this. The DI knew she needed to speak to someone who knew more about investments than she did, as much of the information might as well have been written in a foreign language, but this could be crucial to working out what really happened and why.

A quick Google search told her that you had to be worth a substantial amount – like over a million – to become an accredited hedge fund investor. The average Joe wouldn't qualify.

In the last two weeks of his life, Ben Davies had lost

around fifty-thousand pounds alone, putting him even further into the red. In the last two weeks of his life, Robert Bennett had had nothing left to lose, borrowed or otherwise.

She had a look at the brief info on the hedge fund management firm both men had used: 'Boxhall Investments'. There was a glossy pamphlet attached, which didn't telling her anything much, lacking as it was in the sort of substance Yvonne needed. Clearly, one had to talk to them to find out what they really did.

Another firm they had in common was an independent financial adviser, 'Williams and West'. Their headquarters was in Newtown. She made a note of people to look up and, if she was able, interview.

She was tired. Too tired to continue. It had been an emotionally draining day and she needed her bed. After a mug of hot chocolate, that's exactly where she was.

She knelt down and plucked a couple of weeds from on the grave. Sitting on her heels, she perused the open-book headstone. Black letters on marble. The last testament to her father's existence. She added her flowers to those already placed there by Kim and her children. Her dad would have been fifty-five today.

She mostly remembered him as the happy man of her childhood, hiding the sadder version of him in the deeper recesses of her mind. But she vividly recalled that version now: the lack of words, the frequent sighs, the hunched shoulders and the slowness of him. She imagined holding him tight. Holding and not letting go.

Was that how Ben Davies and Robert Bennett were in their last weeks in this world, all slow and hunched and silent? Not if Kelly, Ben's neighbour, was correct. Not only had he sought help, but he was planning on buying a barge. He'd been attempting to work it through. Had he suddenly just given up? Like her father did when he found out...

Kim had been right, of course. Her mother, though selfishly having an affair, could never have predicted that their father would take the ultimate step. Yvonne wondered that if prior knowledge would have altered her mother's path.

Her thoughts were interrupted by her mobile erupting in her pocket.

"DI Giles."

"Ma'am, it's Dewi. We have a fibre in the rape case. It's not much, but it *is* a fibre from the attacker, we believe, as it was found on the girls undergarments and was not from any of her clothing."

"Well, that's a good result, Dewi, and may help if we find him. Have there been any other developments?"

"Not yet, may have some more when you get back from leave tomorrow."

"Thanks, Dewi." She smiled as she hung up. She knew that Dewi had contacted her to check she was all right. She appreciated it, and was grateful they had a small piece of evidence in their rape case. That was something, at least.

DEBORAH BALL LOOKED FLUSTERED. She shouted something to her children, Yasmin and Michael. Whatever it was, they appeared not to be listening. He adjusted his position so that he could see the mother more clearly. Tony Ball was still at work. He put his binoculars down for a moment. His arms ached.

It was nearly time. There they were, going about their daily routine, whilst he was experiencing the build-up:

becoming more and more tense until he could no longer resist the urge to kill. They had no idea of the coming storm.

He put the binoculars to his eyes once more. She'd disappeared. Where was she? He couldn't see her. He switched from window to window. She must be in another part of the house. No matter, he was familiar enough with her day. He was much more interested in her night.

He watched the children play for a few minutes more. Watched Michael pulling his sister's hair and her screaming out. Watched her chasing him out into the garden and tripping over in the process. Deborah came out to order them to stop it, telling them they'd have to go inside.

Her words either made no difference at all. They paused, only to resume once her back was turned. He put the binoculars back in his bag, took a long cold swig of coke, and left them to it.

BACK AT NEWTOWN CID, the dreaded news awaited Yvonne. They'd closed the Davies case. It was DC Callum who told her, five minutes after she entered the station. Yvonne went straight to Llewellyn's office.

"Can we have a few more days on this, sir? I'm awaiting some forensic results."

"Yvonne, we have all the forensics we need on. More forensics, unless they provide conclusive evidence of another DNA, or similar, are not going to sway the super or the crime commissioner, to resource further investigation."

TONY BALL YAWNED as he left the sofa to go answer the door. He checked the clock: eleven-thirty pm. He was bang on time. Tony appreciated that. You could rely on a man who kept good time, and god knew he needed people he could count on.

"Come in." The words had genuine warmth.

"Where's the family?"

"Fast asleep in their beds." Tony took him through to his study. They'd be private there, at the back of the house. It was a good place to conduct business. He wandered over to the drinks cabinet. "Want one?" He began pouring himself a single malt.

"Not now, maybe later." The other sounded relaxed but firm in his refusal.

"So, why the cloak-and-dagger stuff? Why come here so late?"

"Did you keep it to yourself, like I asked?"

"Yes, of course..."

"How about the wife?"

"Even from my wife. No-one knows. Now, will you tell me what's going on?"

"I think I may be able to help you out of the financial hole you find yourself in."

Tony stared at him. "Really? How?"

"I've got access to some seriously good shorts. Word is, they are going to yield big time in the next few weeks. The time to invest is now."

Tony sighed. "I have nothing. I'm massively in the red. Way beyond investing in anything, my friend."

"What if I were to tell you that I could fund you, at least initially? You could pay me back when you cash in."

"You would fund me?"

"I'm that confident in this trade."

"Insider info?"

"Shhhhh..."

"Hence the cloak-and-dagger, eh?" Tony took him in. He

looked expensive and sleek as a panther, in casual black slacks and black jumper. He usually appeared business-like: a precisely knotted tie, an Italian-styled cotton shirt. The expensive weave of the jacket and trousers, or flash of purple silk, when he opened a jacket up. All of this set off with Italian leather shoes. He had the look of quality. Like he knew how to get what he wanted.

"Could this get me jail time?"

"Sometimes we have to take the plunge. Risk it all."

"I couldn't do that to my family." Tony physically pulled back.

"The chances of anyone doing jail time is minute, most of all for you. It'll be my money we invest, initially. I'll take back my slice, we'll share the profit, and we can reinvest if we choose. Win, win. Do you have a shotgun?"

"You know I do."

"Then get it."

Tony frowned. "Why do I need a shotgun?"

"Look at me."

"I'm looking..."

"What do you see?"

"Well..."

"I need to know you're with me one hundred percent. I need to know I can trust you and that you're up for the challenge. Go get the gun. Make sure it's loaded."

Tony nodded, poured himself another whiskey, and went to fetch the gun from his gun cabinet.

"Is it loaded?"

Tony placed the loaded gun on the table, with a box of cartridges, thinking they may be going into the woods to shoot. "It's loaded."

When the other turned the gun on himself, the ends of

the barrels against his mouth, thumb on the trigger, Tony gasped in surprise.

"It's okay. When I put this gun to my mouth, I know it's yours. I know it's quality and that it's well-maintained. I trust you implicitly. The question is, do you trust me enough, with a potentially *very* lucrative investment, and just a small element of risk?"

"I do."

"Go ahead. Put the end of the gun in your mouth. Put your thumb on the trigger. Feel the adrenaline. Your heart racing. That's what this is about."

Tony hesitated.

"Go ahead. I did."

Tony turned the gun on himself, putting the end to his mouth, thumb on the trigger.

"Can you put it in your mouth? That is the question."

Tony did just that. He was shaking, sweat beading on his forehead.

The other moved in close. "See? You are capable."

Tony didn't see it coming. He was thrown backwards, over on his back. His blood and brain matter on the wall behind.

The killer strode to the door to listen, one eye on the window – a possible escape route. Not a sound from the rest of the house. He put on gloves, took the gun from the dead man, and wiped the trigger clean, using the dead man's thumb to make a fresh print. He took out hospital-issue plastic over-shoes and put them on, proceeding upstairs to the bedrooms. There was enough separation between the rooms to lower the risk of the children waking. He'd known this from weeks of watching.

He found the master bedroom and eased open the door, always ready to run.

She stirred, pushing the sleep-mask up on her forehead, lifting herself in the king-size bed, adjusting in the darkness.

"Robert?"

He watched her for a second before letting off one barrel directly into her chest. She fell backwards and there was no further movement.

He pulled the duvet right back and took out a plastic bottle, scooping up the little blood he could. He then pulled the duvet back up, tucking it under her chin. He replaced the cartridge in that barrel and strode the long corridor, where he finished the children: one barrel each, removing the teddy bear and tiny blanket from them both as they slept. He needed the blood to pool so he could collect it in the atomiser, which he would top-up with a little water, to help it spray.

He returned to the father, shaking the atomiser as he entered the room. He sprayed, liberally, onto Tony's shirt-front, after which he removed the over-shoes before leaving the room.

Once in the garden, he avoided the Ball's one CCTV camera and took off the over-garments. He got into his car, driving with no lights until he reached the main road.

Tony Ball had made it easy. He was a gambler. An addict. Easy prey for a man like him.

9

The phone purred for several seconds. Yvonne shifted her weight from foot to foot, chewing on her fingers.

"Tasha Phillips."

"Tasha, I need your help."

"Yvonne?"

"Hello."

There was a laugh on the other end. "What happened to, 'Hi, how are you? Sorry I haven't been in touch for a while?'"?

"Sorry..."

"It's okay. I'm joking. Are you all right?"

"I'm all right, but a local family may not be if I don't stop a killer. If there is a killer, which there may not be. But I think there is."

"You're making perfect sense."

"Sorry, again, I'm a bit fraught."

"I hear that. How can I help?"

"Whole families are being murdered, either by a stranger or by a male within the family - the father. As far as my colleagues are concerned, it's familial-murder. They're not looking for anyone else."

"And *you* are?"

"I think that a local family, and a family from across the border, were killed by a stranger. I also believe that both families were killed by the same offender."

"What makes you think that?"

"The crime scenes are too neat. Little children sleeping without toys or cuddle-blankets in their beds...I feel foolish now."

"Don't, it's fine. Intuition counts for a lot in your job."

"Also, men who had been financially sound, wealthy in fact, lost everything in the last six months of their lives. What if that was by design? Still feeling foolish, when I say these things out loud. I have the files for both crimes and the financial information makes for good reading, but is hard to decipher without having a financial expert to look through them."

There was a pause at the other end, then: "Yvonne, have you gone maverick on this?"

"Uh huh."

Tasha gave a chuckle. "Why am I not surprised? Well, you might need to find yourself a friendly accountant."

"And a friendly psychologist to help me sift through the case files, and tell me if I'm barking up the wrong tree..."?

"Would you like me to come down?"

"Could you? I mean, you likely won't be remunerated for it. My superiors won't commit any of their budget to the investigation. I can offer you food and board for as long as you're down here, *of course*."

"Well, that sounds like remuneration enough for me."

"Then tomorrow wouldn't be to soon. Please come when you're ready."

. . .

DEWI WAS DEEP IN THOUGHT, chewing his pen and gazing out of the window. Yvonne walked into CID main office. "You okay, Dewi?"

"Yes, ma'am, I'm fine. Was just thinking."

"Did the results come through yet for the swab I gave you?"

"Yes, just got them. Where did you swab? It was definitely blood and, by the looks of it, a mix of Mrs Davies and her daughter. There may have been another profile in there, but it was too badly degraded. They even struggled to confirm the other two profiles."

"I thought that might be the case. I had no way of keeping the sample cold, and the crime scene was already more than forty-eight hours old."

"What are you up to?" Dewi eyed her with suspicion.

"Well, I figured that, if I was correct, and Ben didn't kill his family and himself, then the he would have had to have been killed first. That's the only way the killer could have guaranteed carrying out his plan without incurring too much risk to himself."

"Ma'am, the case is closed. Where did the swab come from, anyway?"

"The underneath of the breakfast bar."

"Are you onto something? Are you going to Llewellyn?"

"It's not enough, Dewi. It couldn't be introduced as evidence as it wasn't kept cold and I'm not SOCO personnel. The crime scene was already old and about to be cleaned. I had to swab then, or lose the chance forever. I just needed to know if I'm on the right track. The fact that there was blood on the underside of the breakfast bar tells me that my scenario is possible. I'll tell Llewellyn, but I already know what he'll say. There's no way this could be included in a file for the CPS."

"Llewellyn's on his way," Dewi warned her.

"Thanks." Yvonne turned to face the DCI.

"Sir, can I have a word?"

The DCI's hair was ruffled, and it looked like he'd been rubbing his eyes. "Yes, of course, I was going to speak to you anyway. Come to my office."

"Are you okay?" Yvonne enquired with genuine concern.

"Difficult meeting with the superintendent and the PCC."

Yvonne followed him down the corridor, mentally preparing for the conversation ahead. She felt guilty for approaching him when he was so obviously in need of a break. She was also afraid of how he might react.

"So." Llewellyn looked directly at her, once he'd closed his office door. "You go first." His smile took her by surprise.

"I went back to the house...before it was cleaned."

"Which house? The Davies's house?" His eyes narrowed and he crossed his arms.

Yvonne nodded. "To the Davies house. You did tell me I could carry on investigating, until the case was officially closed."

Llewellyn glanced at the door and adjusted his tie. "I said if anything came to light, we could investigate it."

"Well, in my book, that's the same thing, isn't it?"

"Go on."

"Well, just supposing I am right and Mr Davies did not kill his family."

"Yvonne, I thought we-"

"Just humour me for a moment, please."

He sighed and nodded.

"If Mr Davies didn't kill his family, someone else did.

That *someone* would have *had* to have taken Ben Davies out first. There's no way he would have risked the man of the house fighting back. A man seeing his family hurt would fight back no matter the risk to himself."

"But Ben Davies had his family's blood on the front of his shirt. That wouldn't have been the case if he died first...unless, you're trying to tell me the blood was planted?"

"Maybe it sounds far-fetched, but yes. That's exactly what I think happened."

"Is there anything in the forensics reports to support what you're suggesting?" The DCI angled his head to one side.

"Not in the official SOCO reports, no sir."

"Right..."

"I have done tests of my own, though, sir." Yvonne pulled a face as though straining to get the words out. "When I went back to the house, I took a swab kit, on a hunch. I drew the swab along the underside of the breakfast bar, where Ben Davies died."

"Could you see blood stains there?"

"Nothing really obvious, just a slight discolouration of the oak. Could have been from anything but, if my thinking was correct, then the killer would have had to spray blood from the family onto Ben Davies' shirt. I felt that that would have to leave a trace, however slight, on the underside of the breakfast bar. The killer would have had to be under there, to spray Ben Davies' shirt front, and it would have been hard for him to control a fine mist."

"I don't see it. Fine mist? Blood that's been hanging around, even for a minute or two, would be too thick to spray a fine mist. Wouldn't it?"

"Yes, but I suspect the killer mixed in a little water from the bathroom."

"Anything to corroborate that?"

"Maybe, in the forensics report they mention one blood spot, around the size of a five-pence piece. It was watery, as though the killer had washed at some point. Except, there were no traces of blood in the plughole. Could it have fallen from a small container?"

"I see what you're saying, but I thought the forensic report supported the pathologists' conclusion that it was murder-suicide?"

"They did. But they make no mention of the underside of the breakfast bar. As far as I can see, they didn't swab it."

"So you gave them a sample."

"Yes, I did." Yvonne held her hand up, as the DCI looked more interested. "One problem, sir: I was in a race against time to swab it before the cleaners moved in. I didn't keep the sample cold, and I had a conversation with Ben's neighbour prior it getting it back here, to be sent off."

"Oh no..."

"I thought it a long shot, and I wasn't really expecting it to lead to results. In any event, by then it possibly made little difference as the scene was already three days old. Some DNA degradation was inevitable. In fact, we were lucky it wasn't all degraded."

"What was the result?" The DCI asked the question but Yvonne could tell that he already felt the evidence to be of little value.

"They confirmed the presence of blood, and of Mrs Davies and her little girl's DNA. There was a partial profile which could have been that of the boy, but it was too degraded to prove absolutely."

"But that DNA could just have easily gotten there in sweat from their fingers?"

"That's right, sir. We can't rule out sweat being in the mix."

"I see..." The DCI was about to turn away.

"The blood droplet in the bathroom sink contained DNA from every family member apart from Ben Davies, in amounts consistent with it being a mixture of their blood. It didn't drip off the father because it would have contained his DNA."

"I thought the boy's DNA was absent."

"From the breakfast bar, but not from the sink droplet."

"You've given me a lot to think about, Yvonne. I'm not sure we can use your swab-test as an argument for investigating the case further. We certainly couldn't introduce it in evidence. You would be destroyed in any court."

"I understand that, but it gives a reason to keep digging."

"The Super is on my back. But I promise to think about it."

"Thank you, sir"

The DCI turned on his heel.

"Err...I thought you wanted to speak to me, sir?"

He turned back. "Oh yes, the rape case. How's that coming along?"

"It's with forensics at the moment. No DNA, but they do have a single fibre, taken from the girl's underwear."

"Did they manage to get a better clarity for the CCTV footage?"

"No, sir."

"So, it hasn't advanced much."

"My team is on the case, sir. They're knocking on doors, asking around. I'm still optimistic."

10

Yvonne opened her door to a beaming Tasha, complete with two large suitcases, two bottles of wine, and a large bunch of yellow lilies.

The DI beamed back. At last, an ally. A co-conspirator. Someone to really bounce ideas off, and someone whose opinion she'd trust, even if that opinion was that she was wrong about the whole thing. They hugged, and she helped carry the cases into the room she'd prepared with fresh linen. They returned to the kitchen to put the lilies in water and pour two glasses of wine. The smell of basil and garlic wafted everywhere, from the lasagne in the oven.

"Something smells amazing." Tasha sniffed the air.

The DI laughed. "I can always rely on you to enjoy my cooking."

"I've missed it." Tasha pulled a face before taking a wandering around the spacious kitchen, with its high ceiling. She stopped at the montage wall.

"Wow. You really have gone maverick, haven't you?"

"I have to admit this isn't your usual montage."

They both now stared at the flow chart and photographs from the Davies family crime scene.

Tasha stood with her head angled to one side. "An emotive scene..."

Yvonne nodded.

"These photographs are yours." It was a statement of fact. Tasha turned to the DI. "You took these."

"How did you know?"

"They're not matter-of-fact crime scene photos. The person who took these was feeling emotional. The close-ups of personal effects. These are not clinical pictures cataloguing deaths. They tell a story. The bodies may be absent from the smears of blood, but I feel as though they are still there."

"I went back to the scene before it was cleared."

"The mum was rising when she was attacked?"

"Yes, I believe so. He killed her and then calmly tucked her back in bed."

"And your superiors think this was a husband showing care, and maybe remorse?"

"Yes, that's exactly what they think."

"But you don't."

"The killer took the children's favourite things from their arms before killing them."

"You're sure about that?"

"Pretty sure, yes. Look at the shelf." Yvonne pointed to the relevant photo. "There they are: cwtch blankets and teddy bears. All removed and placed on the shelf. Why? Then the killer takes their lives and calmly tucks them up in their beds. I believe those two actions are in complete conflict."

"I agree. However, if it was the father, and he was suicidal, he wouldn't be thinking rationally."

"I know that..."

"Do you have pictures from the other crime scene you told me about? The Maesbury case?"

"I do. They are going up next. I have the file on the kitchen island. I have to return it as soon as I can. Officially, I'm off the case. We're not pursuing anything."

"You said you went back to the Davies scene. What were your thoughts?"

"Come with me tomorrow. I'll take you through it."

THE HOUSE, now completely devoid of furnishings, echoed eerily. The DI led the way in and Tasha followed behind, armed with Yvonne's photographs.

"There was no sign of forced entry and no forensic traces, other than those of the family." Instead of going straight upstairs, the DI took Tasha through to the kitchen. "If I'm right, Ben Davies knew their killer. He let him in. A late night caller. The visit had probably been prearranged. Perhaps, a secret business deal."

"Okay, I'm with you so far."

"So, Ben Davies lets the killer in and they discuss their business."

"What about the gun? How did the killer get Ben's gun, without him knowing about it?"

"Made some pretext? Getting a glass of water? Going to the toilet?"

"All gun cabinets are locked. They can't *legally* be otherwise. How'd the killer get hold of the key?"

"Maybe he gets Ben to fetch the gun."

"What reason would he give?"

"Wanting to see it? Compare with one of his own? I can only speculate at the moment. But let's say Ben gets the gun and gives it to the killer to hold. Killer shoots him in the face, while he's sat at the breakfast bar. I think dad died first. My colleagues think mum died first."

"Ben was found in here, slumped on the island." Tasha held up the crime scene photo, as she walked to the breakfast bar.

Yvonne demonstrated the position. "He was folded over, like this, his belly back from the island top and his head slumped on his forearms. If I'm right, the killer came back *after* he had killed the rest of the family and sprayed their blood onto the front of Mr Davies, where he lay slumped."

"A lot of blood sprayed backwards from Ben Davies on the floor and the wall behind."

"I think he had to have been standing, or sitting, at around forty-five degrees to the island top. Killer put the gun in his mouth. Must have ordered him to open it. They think he didn't die immediately. Took a few seconds."

"Mrs Davies may have been woken by the gun going off, but may not have realised that was what had woken her." Tasha pursed her lips.

"Yes. That's what I think. Ben wasn't in bed, and she was wondering where he was. She started getting up, to go take a look, but the killer walked in and blew her away. Then he put her back in bed, tucked her in, and then headed down the corridor to the children's room."

"But he didn't kill them straight away."

"No. Weirdly, he removed their things from their arms, while they slept, and put them on the shelf."

"Why didn't the children wake up at this point?"

"He was gentle. They may have stirred, but not opened their eyes. If my nephew and niece are anything to go by, small children can be difficult to rouse at the best of times."

"So why remove the toys?"

"Beats me. I'm still working that one out."

"Do you think any of the children became aware, before they died?" Tasha shuddered.

"It's hard to say. I hope not. What I can say is that two of them were repositioned after their deaths. And tucked back up."

"Then you think the killer went back downstairs and sprayed theirs and their mother's blood onto the father..."

Yvonne turned her soulful eyes to the door. "Come with me. I'll show you. I think he took blood from the victims, in some sort of household spray gun."

"An atomiser?"

"An atomiser. He then, I believe, walked to the bathroom and added a little water."

"To help it spray, otherwise the blood it too viscous."

"Precisely. He then returns to the kitchen and sprays, from underneath the breakfast bar on the island, onto Ben Davies' shirt-front. Except, that the atomised spray spreads a onto the underside of the breakfast bar. I know, as I swabbed it and had it tested. There was blood from at least three of the other victims."

"Had forensics not swabbed there, themselves?"

"No. Well, given the scenario everyone believed they were looking at, there was no reason to think there would be blood there. All the blood was behind Ben Davies. And his shirt-front wasn't touching the island, when they found him."

"Well, if you're right, we're looking for a confidence trickster. A con-artist able to convince a confident, savvy businessman to give him his gun."

"He may have been a friend. What strikes me is the similarities with the Maesbury case: all victims neatly tucked up;

blood smears, showing the wife and daughter had been moved after death."

"And the father killed with his own gun."

"Right."

"The killer would have been planning these murders for some time."

"I think he may have been stalking his victims. Question is, why? What did he gain? There's no evidence of a sexual interference."

"Well, none that's overt. Doesn't mean there wasn't a sexual motive. He just didn't indulge in physical intercourse. If he was stalking the family, he may have had a sexual pleasure from that, and from the killing, itself."

"Both men were in major financial difficulty. All of it pretty recent. Could the killer have orchestrated that?"

"Have you checked out their business associates?"

"I have a list of most of the people Ben Davies and Robert Bennett had financial dealings with. It's probably not exhaustive, and, to be honest, it's a hell of a task to go through those, alone. And, as for interviewing, how am I going to do that when I'm not supposed to be investigating the case?"

"What about your swabs? Did they not buy you a bit of time?"

"No, headquarters are adamant the case is open-and-shut, regardless of the blood on the underside of the island. It can't be used in court."

Yvonne's mobile made them jump. The DI put a hand to her chest, a look of apology directed towards Tasha. "Yvonne Giles."

"Ma'am, it's Dewi. Where are you?"

"I'm with a friend who might be able to help us."

"Can you meet me at the station? Another family has been killed. The DCI asked if we can go over and check it out. Uniform's first assessment is it's another total wipeout perpetrated by the head of the household."

"Dewi, I'll be right there."

11

Another country residence in the Welsh marches, this time close to Montgomery. Another scene of carnage. Yvonne hadn't yet entered the property, but she knew what she was about to see. She paused at the door to prepare herself. The duty officer gave a knowing look as he signed her in.

"Are you okay, ma'am?" Dewi, having locked the car, was at her side, scrutinising her.

She had to do this. It was part of her job. She had to come and see the scene for herself. But a part of her would be forever changed, as it always was when she witnessed the aftermath of violent death. She nodded. "Let's do this."

DC Clayton was waiting for them in the spacious hallway, illuminated by a huge skylight. "Shall we start with Mrs Ball? She's upstairs."

Yvonne frowned, scanning around. "Where's Mr Ball's body?"

"In his study, ma'am."

"Then I'd like to start there."

DC Clayton raised his brows and shrugged his shoulders at Dewi, who sighed in response. The DI didn't notice. She was already in the doorway to the study. The force of the blast had sent Tony Ball backwards, in same the direction of his blood and brains. He was sat, back to the wall, head bowed forward. The wall behind him was a mess. Blood smeared downwards from several feet above him.

Yvonne put a hand to her mouth and gagged. When she recovered, she mentally compared the scene with the one she'd seen in Knighton. Ben Davies' his high-backed barstool must have blocked the backward force. She believed it was shock she was seeing in the wide eyes of Tony Ball. He hadn't seen it coming.

"What are your thoughts?" Dewi asked from behind.

"That he didn't kill himself. I see surprise in his eyes."

"I think a gun blast can do that, ma'am, even in a suicide."

The DI crackled in her plastic over-suit as she gingerly made her way around the room.

One small glass, with the remains of a whiskey, was taken for analysis by SOCO. "Dutch courage," Dewi stated.

"Or a killer's way of getting the victim relaxed," Yvonne countered.

There were traces of blood on the dead man's shirt front. The DI felt she knew whose blood it would be, though this time Tony's blood would also be present.

There were no obvious signs of a struggle. The window blinds were closed. The light from the SOCO lamps was harsh in its brilliance but, last night, it would have been soft. Dimmed. The sleepy house silent.

"Let's go upstairs." Yvonne steeled herself, stomach muscles clenched tight, as she purposely slowed her breathing.

"Would you like me to go first?" Dewi already had one foot on the stairway.

"Sure."

She put herself in a killer's shoes. If it was as she suspected, he'd already killed Tony Ball when he climbed these stairs. The harbinger of death was in mid-flow and moving swiftly. The noise of the gunshot would most likely have woken Mrs Ball and he couldn't risk getting into a struggle. Couldn't risk leaving traces of himself.

DC Clayton was talking to a SOCO officer. "Ma'am." He nodded, as she brushed past. "Looks like Deborah Ball was sitting up in bed when she was shot. The husband moved her back into bed and tucked her in."

"So, she was awake. There's no evidence she was reading, no bed-time drink in her hand or nearby. Sleep-mask pushed up onto her head. Something woke her. She was listening, ready to get out of bed."

"Or wondering why her husband hadn't joined her yet. Maybe she'd called out to him. Maybe they were arguing." Dewi rubbed his jaw.

"Are you playing devil's advocate, Dewi? Or do you still think I'm reading this all wrong?" The DI's tension was evident in her clipped tone.

"I'm not saying your suspicions are *completely* unfounded, ma'am, but we have no evidence that anyone else was involved." Dewi twisted in his seat, look away and fiddling with his tie.

"Three cases, Dewi. Three cases with remarkably similar circumstances."

Dewi sighed. "Perhaps this will be the case to throw something up, if you're right. *But,* if you're not, you know the superintendent and the DCI will not allow a follow-up."

"I'm prepared for that." The DI sighed too, as she stared

out through the window at the rain which had begun to fall. "?I'm going to ask if I can investigate financial irregularities. Work with fraud office. What are the reasons that a number of wealthy men have suddenly and inexplicably seen their wealth collapse, taken their own lives and those of their families. It's not a given that people in such despair take their loved ones with them. That's rare, most people who kill themselves do it somewhere alone. Somewhere private. They leave a note." Yvonne's eye's glistened with tears she fought to hold back. She was thinking of her father.

Dewi nodded, looking at his shoes.

Yvonne turned to him. "There's something more going on here. It's been a few years since the financial crash. Businesses have been in recovery for a couple of years. I've just got to persuade the powers-that-be to let me look into it."

"They'll ask you to leave it to fraud."

"I'll deal with that bridge when I get to it, Dewi."

Yvonne headed down the corridor to the children's room. It didn't appear they'd known anything about it. If one of them had woken, it didn't show. They were killed where they lay. Neither had moved.

As with their mother, they'd been tucked up. Neither of them had anything in their bed to cuddle. Coincidence, after coincidence, after coincidence. Yvonne felt upset and angry: upset for the children who had not yet known much of life; angry with her colleagues for refusing to see.

"For what it's worth, ma'am, I'm beginning to have doubts about these suicides. If you want some help to do a little...err...moonlighting...I'm up for it."

"Thank you, Dewi." Yvonne's face appeared more relaxed, but it was fleeting. She turned her attention back to the children. She had, once more, an overwhelming urge to scoop them up and hold them to her. Wanted to breathe back the life so violently taken. Turn back time. She thought of her nephew and niece. She would hold them that much tighter the next time she saw them.

That night, she related everything to Tasha, breaking down several times in the telling.

THREE DAYS LATER, and both she and Dewi poured over the early forensics and pathologist's reports. Yvonne was desperate for Tasha to see the murder scene, but would have to wait until SOCO had finished at the house, and visitors were no longer being logged.

Disappointed, though not surprised, there was nothing in the reports to indicate the presence of anyone else at the property, Yvonne put her head in her hands, dejected and riddled with self-doubt. She thought again of her father and of Ben Davies, whose neighbour had described a loving family man who had wanted to take his loved ones far away from it all, to live on a canal barge. Had he changed his mind? And did Tony Ball *really* feel that his family would be better off dead than live without him?

"MA'AM?" DC Clayton held out her milk-no-sugar tea.

"Thank you." She felt exposed.

"Ma'am, regarding the rape case..." DC Clayton waited for it to register. "We've been cross-referencing other rape cases in the area."

"Did you find anything?"

"We did. A case in Maesbury March. Very similar MO. Victim was out with friends. Left the pub alone to walk the quarter-of-a-mile home."

"Did you say Maesbury?"

Clayton checked his notes. "Yes, Maesbury."

"Have you spoken to West Mercia?"

"We've got some of the details already from Shrewsbury CID. I'll put them on your desk. Victim remembered he smelled strongly of soap."

"Just like our perp." Yvonne pursed her lips, tapping a ruler on her hand. "Great. I'll take a look."

It was just what she needed to snap her out of despondency.

DC Clayton joined her to look over the notes, while they waited for Dewi to come back from a dental appointment.

"She left the Navigation Inn at around eleven and headed along the main road. The perp was waiting at the entrance to the canal and dragged her along the tow-path." DC Clayton handed her the papers he had.

"A bit random, waiting there. What if no female came along? Did she walk that way regularly at that time of night? Or had he been watching her in the pub, either from inside or outside?"

"They're still working on it."

"I have a feeling, based on our case, that our perp stalked our victim."

"I'm inclined to agree."

Yvonne tapped her pen on the notes. "So, this happened late April." Frown lines appeared on her forehead. "The Bennetts were killed in mid-May, their house was a couple of miles further down 'Main Road'.

Dewi was back. Yvonne took a deep breath and dived in. "Listen, guys...our victim, Tina Pugh, was raped in Welshpool but works in Montgomery, where the Balls were murdered. This victim...erm...Angela Barnes, was raped on the canal path in Maesbury – where the Bennetts were killed. Quite a coincidence, don't you think?"

"Wow." Dewi leaned in. "That is a coincidence and a half. Are you going to speak to Llewellyn?"

"No, but I do want us to speak to Tina again. If I'm right, and he's choosing, and watching, his victims for some time before pouncing, she may have seen him or met him and not realised it. I don't know, maybe days, maybe weeks beforehand."

"I'll give her a call." DC Clayton headed off.

"Do you think there could be a link?" Dewi leaned back onto the DI's desk, arms folded.

"Maybe, I don't know, Dewi. I'm doubting myself at the moment. Perhaps I'm seeing links where there are none. Suspicious circumstances where there are none."

"Hey... Come on..." Dewi put a hand on her shoulder. "If it helps, I'm beginning to agree with you, and I definitely think we need to talk to Tina. If these rape cases are linked, then our perp is mobile. He may not be local to the areas in which he's attacked. Perhaps he stood out to Tina, if he was a stranger hanging around Montgomery. Chin up. This could be our way in to investigate the potential murders."

Yvonne leaned back in her chair, smiling warmly at her DS. "Thank you, Dewi. That really helps." She meant it.

"Tasha. I need to talk to you." Yvonne arrived home that evening shattered, but her mind was still buzzing. "I've been dying all day to talk to you about the case."

"The downside to having no mobile signal out in the country." Tasha laughed. "What is it?"

"Could a killer getting his kicks from murdering families, also be a rapist of non-related females?" Yvonne threw her bag down in the hall and headed towards the kitchen, where she could smell something wonderful cooking.

"Well, it's possible, of course. If you're asking whether the murderer in your case is a rapist. Well, that would depend on his motivation. Just supposing you're right, and a murderer of families is also raping, I'd say his motivations for the murders might also be sexual. I did say to you I thought that might be the case at the Davies house."

"Yes, I know you did. I was keeping an open mind."

"What if he was sexually attracted to a female in the family. He may have met the family socially, or through work, and liked the mother. Sexual predators do not always interfere sexually with their victims. As you know, some use a knife as a surrogate penis. Others, well, they get their satisfaction from the power they feel: control over life and death. And, of course, the stalking and watching is stimulating for them."

"So, then would they actually rape, if that's not what gets them off?"

"Well, what if he really wants to rape the mothers? What if that's what he would do, given the choice. He can't do that because you guys would know it wasn't a familial-homicide."

"So he rapes someone else, not connected. Maybe when he's been stalking the female he does want?" The penny dropped for Yvonne.

"Bingo. He may even want the other females too, but the chances are they are just available and unconnected to the perp. In which case, any young female could be a target."

"I want to take you to the Ball's house in Montgomery. SOCO should be finishing up there tomorrow. We're also going to talk to Tina Pugh, a rape victim who *works* in Montgomery. It's not where she was raped, but what if our murderer was stalking the Balls and saw Tina and decided to follow her..."

"If you're right, we've got a complex perp. A sophisticated operator with spare time on his hands."

"Yeah, I'm still figuring the spare time thing out."

12

Dewi and Yvonne stood outside of Tina's cafe, the Castle Kitchen, in Montgomery. They'd arrived early, just after she'd opened up. Before the first customers arrived.

Tina greeted them at the door. Yvonne was reminded of her tiny stature. She would have offered little resistance to the attacker.

"Is this okay?" Yvonne asked, placing a hand on Tina's arm.

"Yes, I thought now would be best. We're not officially open for another half an hour. The owners are away on holiday, so I'm working longer hours to cover everything."

"We wanted to ask you about the weeks leading up to the attack on you."

"Okay." Tina pulled some chairs out from underneath the table and they all sat down.

"Had you noticed anyone following you? Anyone paying you more attention than usual?"

"Umm...not really."

"How about here in the shop? Anyone start coming on a regular basis who wasn't your regular customer? Someone who has stopped coming in now?"

"Ummm no, not really. We cater for a lot of tourists. They are almost always strangers."

"Anyone who stood out to you for any other reason?" Yvonne pulled a face. Was she sounding desperate?

"Don't think...no...wait. Yes, yes there was someone."

Yvonne and Dewi looked at each other then back at the girl.

"Who?" Dewi asked.

"Some guy did upset me. He implied that I was nothing, for no reason. Seemed really full of himself."

Yvonne leaned in towards Tina. "Tell me about him."

"He ordered something...a snack and a drink, or something, I don't remember what at the moment. He was casually dressed but it was very smart casual, if that makes sense. He was wearing a flat cap. I remember that. And he didn't take it off."

"What else was he wearing?"

"Wax jacket; shirt; Jumper Jeans or Casual trousers. His trousers were dark in colour. Sorry, I have so many people come in, I'm struggling with the detail."

"How did he upset you? In what way did he imply you were nothing?"

"It was the conversation. He was sat over on that table." Tina indicated the place, opposite.

"Do you mind if I sit there for a moment?" Yvonne pushed her chair back.

Tina shook her head. "Go ahead, be my guest."

The DI sat at the table, facing the girl and Dewi. Behind them was the fireplace and, to her right, the door into the food preparation room. She wondered what he might have been thinking.

"What did he say to you?"

"I was making small talk. I can't remember the exact words. I asked him if he was here on vacation. He answered that he was. I asked him what he did, and it was his answer that was pretty mean, actually."

"What was it?"

"He said he did money, and implied I wouldn't know what that was. Implied that I had nothing. I can't remember his exact words, but he had this look on his face. It made me feel small and insignificant."

"He said he *did* money?" Yvonne searched the girl's face. The DI's mind was racing. Money. Something in common with the dead families. "How long was he here for?"

"Twenty minutes? Not much more than that. He left right after a family came in. He seemed irritated, maybe by the children who were very lively."

"Did you see which direction he..."

"Tea!" Tina announced. "He had Darjeeling tea."

"Did he say where he was from?"

"No. At least, I don't remember if he did."

"And which direction did he head in when he left?"

"I was busy with the family. I'm sorry. I didn't see."

"That's okay, Tina."

Yvonne and Dewi finished up by asking Tina how she was, and making sure she was receiving after-care from police, SARC, and victim support personnel.

"Interesting..." Dewi rubbed his chin as they walked away from the cafe, towards their car just off the square. "He said he did money."

"I know." Yvonne looked directly at her DS. "Maybe I'm

making connections that aren't there, but money is an obvious link with the dead families."

"I can feel myself gravitating to your position." Dewi grinned at her. "If this is madness, it's *very* infectious."

13

"I could get used to this."

Yvonne threw her bag down in the hall and threw her coat on a peg. The smell of curry, wafting from the kitchen, made her realise just how hungry she was, and she breathed deeply of the rich aroma.

Tasha appeared from the kitchen, two glasses of chardonnay at the ready.

Yvonne sipped and gave a relaxed sigh. "It's been a busy day. This is just what I need."

"I've been pretty busy, too." Tasha smiled back.

"I know. I can smell. I didn't mean to..." Yvonne grimaced in embarrassment.

"It's okay. I didn't mean the cooking." Tasha laughed. "I meant I've been studying the files and digging out anything I could on the financial players involved with your dead families."

"You've been doing that?" Yvonne's face lit up as though the sun had peeked out from behind the clouds.

"I certainly have, and I have my notes, some Google results, and some ideas to throw at you after dinner. You have to eat first. Come to think of it, so do I. Can't think on an empty stomach."

"Happy for that, I'm ravenous."

Yvonne walked with Tasha through to the kitchen. She was impressed with how clean and tidy the kitchen looked. The curry had been prepared from fresh ingredients, judging by the pile of peels and vegetable ends ready for the compost, but it was evident that Tasha was someone who cleaned up as she went. A complete contrast to the DI, who tidied afterwards – sometimes the next day.

The psychologist looked cool and calm, wearing a white cotton shirt which was remarkably untouched by cooking splashes. Yvonne felt genuine admiration.

After a bowlful of curry and a naan bread each, they got down to business.

"So, what have you found out?" Yvonne perused Tasha's notes, as the other finished her wine.

"First thing that struck me was that both Davies and Bennett were investors in the same hedge fund, a...'Boxhall Investments', based in London. Rob Bennett was using a fairly local financial advisory firm, and we can find out if the same firm was also involved with Ben Davies." The psychologist cracked open the Bennett file. "Here's what we've got regarding Bennett's investments - hedge firms, brokers, financial advisers."

"Do we have more info on Boxhall Investments?"

"Not a huge amount in here, no." Tasha grabbed her laptop and tapped the space bar. The screen lit up. "Here's what's online. This is the company website, and there's the CEO, Mark Grantham. I spoke with a friend at the Met, and apparently this firm was investigated a few years ago by the Serious Fraud Office: suspected insider trading. At least one of the employees was fired, but although they suspected

Mark Grantham of heavy involvement in the illicit trades, nothing could be pinned on him."

Yvonne stared at the picture of Mark Grantham. His picture loomed large on the front page of the glossy website. It was only a photograph, but Yvonne saw a smooth operator. His suit jacket and tie appeared to shimmer in the photographer's light. Their colour coordinated perfectly with the pale-blue designer shirt. He looked like he could do anything and everything with ease. A force of nature. Smart and confident. The kind of man you'd give your last penny to if he told you he could turn it into a fiver.

A loud banging on the front door interrupted their thoughts. Yvonne looked apologetically at Tasha. "So sorry, I forgot. Dewi's joining us for a couple of hours."

Tasha shrugged. "If you're sure..."

"He's coming round to my way of thinking." Yvonne got up to let him in.

He'd brought with him a chinese take out and offered the others some.

"No thanks." Yvonne smiled. "We've just eaten, but I can get you a plate and some cutlery."

"Just a fork, if that's okay. What are you looking at?"

While the DI fetched the fork, Tasha brought Dewi up to speed, laughing at him when he told her it'd been a few years since he had last moonlighted, and that the DI was a bad influence.

"Who was the employee who was fired from the company? The one pinned for the insider trading? Do we know?" Yvonne handed Dewi his fork.

"He's..." Tasha hunted through her notes. "Ryan Smith."

"Do you think this company stole money from the dead businessmen?" Dewi asked between mouthfuls. "If so, why are we looking at someone who is no longer part of the company?"

"Revenge is a powerful motivator." Tasha tapped a couple of links and brought up a photograph and a few details for Ryan Smith. "Looks like he started his own company, albeit much smaller than Boxhall Investments: 'Highland Finance'. I'm guessing so-named because the headquarters are in Edinburgh. If he was hacked-off at getting the push, he might have wanted to get back at the company or its clients."

"Why Edinburgh?" Yvonne stared at the fair-haired man on the screen. "Is Smith *from* Scotland?"

"Don't know. I can try and find out, but I'm guessing that it's cheaper to have their main office there and a small subsidiary in London."

"How was he able to start up a new company if he was prosecuted for insider trading?" Yvonne leaned back on the sofa.

"He wasn't prosecuted. According to my friend in the Met, there wasn't enough evidence. The company let him go to show it was cleaning house. *And* there'd been a fall-out between Grantham and Smith. Again, no-one really knows what that was about, and the two of them certainly didn't want anyone to know."

"Perhaps they have enough dirt on each other to ensure their mutual silence." Dewi cleaned up the rest of his Chinese and placed the empty carton on the coffee table.

"Who are the other players?" Yvonne turned to Tasha. "The financial advisers?"

"Well, that's interesting, too. Both Davies and Bennett were using a firm based in Shropshire. A family firm called 'Williams and Wells.'"

"One family?"

"Family plus associates, from what I've read. Again, we have some info in the files. I did a little digging online to flesh it out. I need to type my notes, so they're legible."

"Okay." Yvonne scribbled on Tasha's notepad. "We can interview the head of 'Williams and Wells' and maybe talk to the fraud office at the Met. Anything they can give me, regarding their investigations. I'd like to know if anyone from either of those companies was in our locality, around the time of these deaths. Holidays or work, doesn't matter." Yvonne paused for breath. "There's something else. I received a cryptic email from DC West, Shrewsbury CID. Something tells me that he wasn't entirely convinced Rob Bennett killed himself and his family. What we need is something...anything...that will convince our superiors to open up the investigation properly. Even if we ultimately discover they were suicides, I need to feel that we completed a thorough investigation. I think we owe the families that much."

14

The first thing to strike the DI, on the approach road to Montgomery, was the castle ruins. Set upon a massive plug of rock, it towered over the tiny town, a weathered and broken testament to the turbulent past of the Welsh Marches.

The town itself lay drizzled over the hillside and, it seemed to Yvonne, the only flat area was the town square. The roads and lanes were steep and narrow. They had difficulty negotiating them through the traffic, it being the busy summer season.

She decided to park in a newly vacated slot, just outside of the Dragon Hotel. They looked around for somewhere to eat their sandwiches. It just wouldn't feel right to eat anywhere near the Balls' home.

Tasha nodded towards the castle. "Why don't we eat up there? Take half an hour out."

Yvonne thought about it. Could they? She was supposedly revisiting Tina Pugh's cafe and having a look around. DCI Llewellyn didn't know she was going to the Ball's again. He'd start to wonder what was taking so long.

In the end, the DI nodded. It was lunch time. She was entitled to a little time out. "Come on then. Let's do it. Half an hour tops, though. They'll start calling me, before too long."

Yvonne could feel the sweat building on her forehead and the small of her back as they meandered up the narrow road.

The ruins themselves were well-maintained, and a large wooden bridge allowed access to the castle's inner sanctum. The view from the top took their breath.

Below them, stretching as far as they could see, were peaceful fields full of colour, and yet more hills in the distance. The sky was busy with billowing cloud of every shade of grey and white. Shards of deep blue permeated the spaces between. The DI felt the tension leave her, and she looked over at Tasha who appeared just as relaxed.

"Can we see the Balls' house from up here?" Tasha wandered over to a piece of wall facing the way they'd come in and peered down at the houses.

The DI climbed up the stones, to get a better view. "I think so. I believe that's it there." She pointed to it. "That large red-brick house, surrounded by its own land, with the tall trees at the back."

Tasha took out her mobile phone and took some pictures.

"Having an idea?" Yvonne smiled at the psychologist, who was shielding her phone from the sun, as she zoomed in on one of the photos.

"Just wondering if your killer might have come up here. Might have watched the house from here. Look, you can see virtually every window at the front."

"Binoculars?"

"Or a spotting scope, something like that. At night, with the lights on, you would see pretty much everything."

Yvonne shuddered. "Are you still thinking the motive might be sexual?"

"Entering a home is a very personal thing. I suspect an underlying sexual motive, but I'm still trying to keep an open mind."

"The wives?"

"We don't know what transpired between him and them, in the semi-darkness. Did he allow them to become aware of his presence? We know they were moved from the precise position they were killed. Tucked back in bed. We don't *really* know whether he talked to them or gave them any instruction. It's just a thought that he might have done those things."

"Surely, that would have been to have risked waking the children?"

"A brief moment of listening would have told him if the children had woken."

"Shall we eat?" Yvonne felt an urgent need to get to the house.

After sandwiches and orange juice, they were on their way back down the hill into the tiny town. A ten minute car ride and they were entering the driveway to the Balls' house.

Police tape still stretched across the pathway and door. Yvonne pushed it to one side. "SOCO finished here yesterday. I wanted to bring you to the house before the relatives come. Wanted you to see it as it was left."

"Can we go around the back?"

"Sure."

"I mean before we go inside."

Yvonne nodded and led the way along the pathway to the right hand side of the house.

"Beautifully kept lawn."

Tasha walked over to the large ash and cherry trees at the back. They passed a large set of swings, a slide and a trike, which lay just as it had been left, on its side, probably there, as the little ones headed in for their tea.

Tasha put a gentle hand on Yvonne's shoulder. "Are you okay?"

She knew the nod she gave Tasha would be unconvincing and she looked away, towards a whirligig in an exposed part of the garden. "Do you suppose he watched the children play? Watched Deborah Ball putting her washing out?"

"That's why I came back here." Tasha pointed to the large but well-kept hedges. "He could have been hiding anywhere here. He wouldn't be seen from the road, or the house, and there are gaps in several places large enough for him to watch undisturbed. This is where he studied them. Learned their routines. He had to have done that."

"And what if my hunch is wrong? What if these were murder-suicides?"

"You suspect intruder-murders, and the reasons you've given me are sound. I'm happy for us to continue. Let's go inside."

It was clear that the Balls had carried out extensive alterations inside the house. The Victorian front facade belied the ultra-modern, light and airy, interior.

"Where do you want to start?" Yvonne asked the psychologist.

"Where would you like me to start?"

"The study, it's where Robert Ball was found and, if my suspicions are right, he would have been killed first. I've got the crime scene photos with me, for you to compare."

They walked through to the spacious study, with its bi-folding glass doors. They looked out over the patio and grounds.

"Robert Ball could have been studied by a prowler quite easily." Tasha took the photos from Yvonne and started looking around.

"So, the gun and ammunition was Robert's," she said, eventually, scratching her head and crouching where Robert Ball had been found.

"Confirmed."

"And he had his family's blood on his shirt front."

"Yes, on the desk you can see brochures about canal barges. His neighbour told me he'd been contemplating taking his family away on a canal trip, with a view to sussing out whether they could live that way. He wanted a life-style change."

"Permanent?"

"That was the idea."

"Doesn't sound like a man who wanted to commit suicide to me."

"No, it doesn't."

"So, how did the killer persuade Robert Ball to take out his gun and ammunition?"

"Apparently, Robert regularly went pheasant shooting, at Bettws Hall, in Bettws village. It's not very far from here – about twenty minutes by car. Apparently, the hall and it caters for some fairly rich clientele, some of whom fly in via helicopter, just for a weekends shooting."

"Getting more interesting."

"It just might be that our killer is one of them."

"Someone very wealthy, maybe someone Robert Ball aspired to emulate. That *could* be a persuasive enough influence."

"Like maybe the CEO of a hedge fund company?"

"Perhaps."

Yvonne took the psychologist around the rest of the house. Tasha took her time, saying little else. By the time they left, Yvonne could tell that she was already formulating her profile.

"Twice in one month. Is something wrong, sis?" Kim stood, one hand on her hip, the other carrying a washing basket.

"Everyone keeps asking me that." Yvonne sighed and took her sister's hand. "I'm fine, honestly. I just wanted to check on you and the kids."

"Tough case?"

"You could say that, but it's not something I want to discuss, if that's all right."

Kim smiled warmly at her sister and wrapped her free arm around her shoulders. "Come on in. The kids will be over the moon."

Yvonne helped Kim prepare dinner: chilli, chips and ketchup. The children whooped as they came running to the dinner table.

Yvonne laughed. "I take it you guys like chilli?"

The sound of forks on plates and talking-with-mouths-full was confirmation enough.

Yvonne watched the easy madness and thought, not for the first time that week, that she was glad her sister was not married to a rich businessman.

Cuddling the children to bed, and reading their bedtime stories, had even more meaning tonight. She held them just that little bit tighter.

"Mum's been asking about you, again." Kim handed her a cuppa as she sat down on the sofa.

"Has she? I will speak to her at some point."

"You said that last time."

"I find it hard."

"I know you do. Look, I can dial in on my laptop. You could speak to her now."

"Will he be there?"

"She loves you."

Yvonne sighed. Life was too short. If she hadn't realised it before, she was realising it now. She nodded to her sister and began clearing her throat.

HER MUM LOOKED OLDER. There was quite a bit more grey in her shoulder-length hair. Yvonne could see herself in twenty years time. She'd inherited her looks from her mother. There was a twinkle in the older woman's eyes. She was clearly excited at the opportunity of speaking to her oldest daughter. But Yvonne also sensed a nervousness.

Kim ruffled her sister's hair and left the room.

"Mum." Yvonne cleared her throat again.

"Yvonne, we've missed you."

"We?"

Her mother ignored the last. "How have you been?"

The DI felt like closing the lid on the laptop. She couldn't do this. Not now.

Her mum talked quickly, wanting to fill the silent void. Perhaps she sensed her daughter's urge to run. Yvonne's reticence must have been palpable.

"We've been decorating the house. If I look like I've been painting myself, that'll be why." The mild Aussie accent seemed wrong on her mother. It served only to emphasise the distance between them. The distance caused by the interloper.

"Talk to me...please." Her mother had the familiar look of despair.

Yvonne felt a massive pang of guilt. She'd missed her mum. She began to cry. Soft sobs. She should have closed the laptop when she had a chance.

"I love you, Yvonne."

"I love you, too. I wish you were here."

A minute passed. Both of them silent. Perhaps her mum was also feeling overwhelmed.

"I visited dad's grave the other day."

"You did?" Her mum's face lit up.

"Yes." Yvonne wiped her eyes with her hand.

"I miss him too, Yvonne," her mum said softly. "It took me a long time to forgive myself."

"Did you ever feel afraid of him? Before he took his life, I mean."

Her mum's wide eyes showed she was genuinely taken aback. "No. Why do you ask that?"

"He would never have hurt us, would he?" It was a statement more than a question.

"Your father loved you more than anything. He loved me too." Anne lowered her eyes. "If anyone hurt us, it was me."

"How's Bob?" That was the first time Yvonne had ever asked her mother about her step-dad.

"He's fine. He asks about you. We've been talking about visiting the UK."

"I've got to go." Yvonne had a lot to think about. She needed time.

"Yvonne?"

"Yes?"

"Don't leave it so long next time..."

Yvonne nodded. "I'll try not to."

. . .

Yvonne braced herself, as she and Dewi entered the police station in Monkmoor, Shrewsbury. She had no idea how this was going to go. DC Dave West, and DS Shaun McAllister from West Mercia police had agreed to meet them, and she'd also have an option to speak with the Oswestry rural south team, who routinely policed Maesbury March.

"Thank you for agreeing to see us." Yvonne took the seat offered by DS McAllister. McAllister appeared to be a seasoned detective in his late forties and West, a good deal younger, maybe thirty. Yvonne mused that West had probably been in the force less than ten years and CID, less than five.

"How can we help?" It was the DS who addressed her, as DC West and Dewi came over with the teas, coffees, and a pack of chocolate digestives.

"We wanted to talk to you about two of your cases. The first is the rape of Angela Barnes in Maesbury Marsh. The other case was the familial-homicide of the Bennetts, also in Maesbury Marsh. You kindly lent me the file." Yvonne sensed intense interest from DC West. From the corner of her eye, she'd seen him lean in, and turned to face him directly. "DC West..."

"Dave, please..."

"Dave, I know you worked on the Bennett case, and I've spoken to you briefly over the phone."

West shifted uncomfortably in his seat and Yvonne didn't mention the cryptic email, guessing it could lead to trouble for the junior detective.

"Did either of you have doubts as to whether the father was responsible for the family's destruction?"

DS McAllister appeared confident. "No, there was nothing to suggest anybody else's involvement. Robert Bennett had lost a considerable amount of money and had been to see his doctor a few times in the weeks before his death. He was suffering from depression and had been a good deal less sociable in the last month or so of his life."

Yvonne looked again at Dave West. He didn't look so sure. He looked as though there was something he'd like to say but was holding back.

The DI changed tack. "Can I come back to that case in a minute? You know we've had two very similar cases to yours, and in a worryingly short period of time."

McAllister nodded. "I understood you'd closed those cases..."

Yvonne bit her lip. "My superiors closed the cases, and they may have been right to do so. I just have some concerns I need to put to rest. I also wanted to talk to you about the rape of Angela Barnes."

"Yes, that was a strange business." McAllister frowned. "A very unusual crime in such a quiet community. The victim insists she does not know who the perpetrator was, suggesting he came from outside of the community."

"And you have a problem with that?"

"Well, how would an outsider have known he'd have a victim that evening? No-one noticed anyone unusual in the pub that night, which would mean the perp was hanging around the canal area on the off-chance. Just doesn't seem very likely."

"Unless the stranger knew her movements." Yvonne took sipped her tea.

McAllister shook his head. "He'd have had to have watched her, or been in the area for a while: days, even weeks."

"What if he was?" Yvonne began dunking a biscuit.

"Where's this leading? Have you got an idea?"

Yvonne looked at Dewi and back, chewing on her

biscuit. She swallowed. "We had a rape in Welshpool with a similar MO: method of abduction; clothing; what he was wearing; and a strong smell of soap."

"Ah yes, of course, the rape in Welshpool."

"That's right, the victim works in Montgomery."

"Okay..." McAllister shook his head, indicating he wasn't making the same connections.

"One of our familial-homicide cases was just outside of Montgomery."

The penny dropped. "Are you suggesting that the rape cases and the family deaths are related?"

"I don't know. It's something I'm considering. Our rape victim, Tina Pugh, stated that a guy had come into her cafe and been extremely rude to her. When she asked him what he did, he replied, 'Money', and then went on to imply that she wouldn't know what that was."

"Nice man," Dave West murmured.

"Quite," McAllister agreed." But that doesn't make him a rapist. Anything else to connect him to the girl? Was he in Welshpool?"

"We don't know."

"What vehicle was he driving?"

"We don't know that either. Tina didn't see him drive away."

"That's a shame." McAllister leaned back in his chair. "The day before Angela Barnes was raped, a silver Lexus was seen hanging around in the lanes. The postman remembered it."

"Did he get a reg?"

"Unfortunately not, and it hasn't been seen since."

"What about when the Bennetts died? Did anyone see an unusual vehicle around at the time?"

"Not that I know of."

"Did you ask?" Yvonne didn't mean it to sound accusatory, and could have kicked herself when she saw the McAllister's lips tighten. She needed these men on-side. "I didn't mean that the way it sounded. I know you wouldn't necessarily be asking those questions if you felt you were dealing with murder-suicide. I just asked in case you had."

Mcallister's gaze softened. "I agree with you, that we are pretty much certainly dealing with the same perp as regards the rapes. There are too much similarities in the descriptions, and the soap-thing stands out."

Yvonne nodded, hopefully.

"Where I don't yet see a connection is with the family deaths. For me, that's a leap too far. Interesting, but not backed up with anything concrete."

"But you said yourself that this rape case was extremely unusual, and that the perp was quite possibly from out of the area, and may have been hanging around. What if it was because he was watching the Bennetts?"

"You've given us something to think about..." McAllister looked away as he said it.

Yvonne finished her tea. "You'd begun looking into the backgrounds of some of the firms Robert Bennett was dealing with, before his death. Could we have what you've got?"

"We didn't uncover anything significant, there. He was a shrewd businessman. His downfall was his tendency to gamble recklessly from time to time."

"On the stock market?"

"Yep."

McAllister was closed. Yvonne knew it. She suggested another cuppa and stayed Dewi with her hand, as he made to get up to go help DC West. "It's okay, Dewi. I'll go. You can continue talking to the DS. Find out more about those firms."

Dave West filled the kettle and put it on its stand.

"Dave...I sense that you wanted to say something back there. Was it about the deaths of the Bennetts?"

Dave searched her face. He was clearly fighting with himself.

"I won't say anything to McAllister. I promise."

"Well, it's just that the scene was too neat. Too organised. Desperate men do desperate things. Here was the ultimate desperate act by an ultimately desperate man."

"Poetic." Yvonne smiled.

Dave grinned back but his eyes were still earnest. The scene should have been disorganised. Rob Bennett was pretty laid back. His study was awash with paper and collections. Nothing laid out neatly. Yet, the murder scene was left all neat and tidied up. Even the children's teddy bears, all lined up on the shelf *very* neatly. Mother and children all tucked up. That's not the disorganised act of a desperate man. That's more like the act of someone very organised."

"You been on training recently?"

Dave grinned. "Does it show?"

"Yes, but that's a good thing." Yvonne was silently thrilled. His intuition had been the same as her own.

CALLUM WAS WAITING FOR HER, when she and Dewi returned to Newtown CID.

"Ma'am, I've been following up on a rape which happened in Llandrindod Wells around two months ago. I think there's a chance it's linked to the rape in Welshpool."

"Wow." Yvonne signalled for Callum to walk with her. "What are the specifics?"

"The victim works in a service station in Llanbadarn Fynydd. She'd just finished a late shift and was on her way home. A friend gave her a lift into Llandrindod Wells and she was walking home. She was pulled off the lane into a field. The perp was wearing a mask. Victim remembers a silver car passing her minutes before but cannot remember more about the car other than it was silver."

"Does she remember anything else about the attacker?"

"No, ma'am."

"Good work, Callum."

"I told her you might want to call on her. She said she was happy for a visit or a telephone call. She stated she just wants him caught before he does it to someone else."

"Thank you." Yvonne felt hopeful. It hadn't escaped her notice that this rape happened within reasonable distance of Knighton – the place where the Davies family lost their lives. If she could show a demonstrable link between this and the other two rapes, she could go back to the DCI.

SARAH EVANS, an articulate young woman, gave detailed answers to each of the DI's questions, over the phone. Yvonne knew that CID from Llandrindod were already on the case, so her questions were few and to the point.

"What do you remember about the attacker, besides what he was wearing?"

"He was medium build, seemed like he worked out. He was strong."

"Did he have an accent?"

"He didn't speak. He grunted and used his strength to defeat me."

"Was there a smell? A scent?" The DI trod carefully, she didn't wish to put words in Sarah's mouth.

"I don't recall."

"Sweat?"

"No, definitely not sweat. He was clean."

"You sound sure about that. How do you-"

"Soap. He smelled of an expensive soap. Like he'd just showered. I don't know how I could have forgotten that."

"Would you recognise the brand?"

"No, but I thought there might have been a hint of something like sandalwood. Yes, I'd say sandalwood. Does that help?"

"It just may." Yvonne was smiling at the phone. "Sarah, I can't thank you enough for speaking to me. I know you will have had a number of interviews already. I'll keep your liaison team posted."

"I just want him caught."

"I know." It was a almost a whisper, before the DI put down the receiver. She instructed DC Jones to pass on the new information to the team in Llandrindod, and headed down the corridor to DCI Llewellyn's office.

15

She gave his door a couple of firm raps.

"Come in."

Was that a good mood 'come in'? Yvonne pushed the door open, quietly clearing her throat. "Good morning, sir."

"Yvonne, good morning to you, too." Llewellyn smiled warmly. "What can I do for you?" He leaned back in his chair, giving the DI his complete attention.

"I've come to ask again if I can investigate the deaths of the Davies and the Ball families."

"I see... Haven't you got enough on your hands investigating the rape in Welshpool? I'm given to understand there's a potentially related rape in Llandrindod Wells?"

Yvonne didn't blink. "Plus another, in Maesbury March. Though that one is not in my jurisdiction. I'm collaborating with Shaun McAllister and Dave West, from West Mercia."

"So, not only do we have a serial rapist, but we have a very mobile one."

"I believe so."

"So, what is this about the family murders again? I thought we'd agreed..."

"I didn't agree, exactly. I did as I was told. I'm not complaining," Yvonne added quickly. "There's something I need to run past you, and it might just change your mind."

"Go ahead. You certainly look excited about something."

"It's the locations, Chris. Can I put this on your desk?" She began unfolding the map she'd brought.

"Be my guest."

"This is the border area. Llandrindod Wells, Maesbury March and Welshpool are all ringed with blue marker. Ringed with red, are Knighton, Maesbury March and Montgomery."

"Okay..." The DCI studied the highlighted areas.

"You're looking at the rape locations in blue and the family deaths in red. What strikes you?"

"Are you telling me you think the rapes and the deaths are related?"

"That's exactly what I'm telling you." Yvonne straightened up, hands on hips. "Each one of the rapes occurred in the periods leading up to the family deaths, and in a similar or same location."

"I have to admit, that is quite striking, Yvonne."

"Isn't it just?"

"Still..."

"Tina Pugh describes a man as having gone into her cafe in Montgomery with what seemed to be an intent to antagonise her. That was a few days prior to her rape. She stated that the man specifically said 'money', when she asked him what he did."

"Did she remember anything else about him?"

"Unfortunately not, she remembered very little aside

from the way he made her feel and the general cut of his clothing."

"It's interesting, but I don't know if that's enough to..."

"There are a lot of interconnected characters, from the world of finance, who interacted with both Davies and Ball. One of the might be involved in the rapes and, I believe, deaths. Each of the victims vividly remembers the perp smelling of soap. One specifically believed it to be an expensive soap, possibly containing sandalwood."

"How easy would it be to combine these investigations? Could your team manage it?"

"There's a lot of potential overlap."

The DCI's eyes twinkled at her. "I'll talk to the super."

"Really?"

"You'll have to keep it hush-hush from the media. I do not want them knowing we are looking into the family deaths unless you find something concrete, that points to stranger-murder. I'll let you know later today or tomorrow if you have the official go-ahead."

"That's great, sir, thank you." Yvonne smiled broadly at him. "I'd be able to officially interview some of the bigger players involved in the businessmen's money-world."

"I *do* value your judgement, Yvonne. Your instincts are first-rate. But please wait until I give you the official nod."

"I will, sir."

"And remember to keep quiet as regards the media. Tell your team."

"Thanks, again."

Yvonne was tempted to skip down the corridor to tell the team, and she couldn't wait to let Tasha know there was now at least a chance of a proper investigation.

. . .

THE WHOLE TEAM was on tenterhooks, waiting for confirmation from Llewellyn. When it came, Yvonne and Dewi set to work, planning the most important next moves.

Dewi confirmed with Bettws Hall that Mark Grantham was a regular visitor and that he travelled up from London in either his private jet or helicopter. He would always land at Welshpool airport.

That he was wealthy was self-evident, but further confirmation was the fact that his regular home was in London's infamous Connaught Square. The knowledge that they were soon to interview the man made Dewi nervous.

"Tread carefully, ma'am. Men like that are more powerful than prime ministers."

"I'm not afraid of him, Dewi." Yvonne grinned. "In fact, I'm relishing the prospect."

"I'm a big fan of your guts." Dewi grinned back at her. "But, even so."

THEY'D AGREED to see him at the airport, for reasons of privacy, since it was only an informal interview. He had not one, but two, legal advisers in tow.

The aircraft hanger had a cool, draughty feel.

"Mark Grantham?" Yvonne held out her hand.

He stared at it for a moment, like he wasn't going to shake it. "Yes, I'm Mark Grantham. You said this wouldn't take long." He grabbed the offered hand, turning it such that his palm was towards the ground.

Yvonne twisted their hands back to a neutral position. "It won't." She waited for Dewi to signal he was ready to take notes, then: "How often do you come to mid-Wales?"

"Oh, let's see...six, eight, ten times a year?"

"What's the nature of your business here?"

"I thought you'd know that. You're surely not coming into this *cold*."

"I'm not going to put words into your mouth, Mr Grantham."

"Mark, please..."

"Mark."

"Well, it's mostly to hunt game or pheasant-shoot. I do talk to business clients in this region, though. So I kill two birds with one stone." He looked directly into her eyes. She felt uncomfortable.

"Do you come alone? Do any of your team accompany you?"

"I sometimes bring my team out here for team-building weekends and outdoor pursuits. That's usually just once or twice a year."

"I see."

"This is all very mysterious. Why would police officers in Mid-Wales want to question me?"

"We're clearing up loose ends around the suicides of businessmen in the area. I understand you knew the two men who died: Benjamin Davies and Tony Ball. I'm talking to *anyone* who had dealings with them. We want to know what drove them to kill themselves and bring closure for the relatives."

Mark Grantham ran his left hand through his slick hair, placing the other on his hip. He appeared every inch confident in his smart-but-casual shirt and jeans. Everything about him screamed expensive. He was tweezed. "That was a bad business." He sighed, flicking a look at one of his advisers, who had so far kept quiet.

"It was," Yvonne confirmed, in a firm but even tone. "Made worse by the fact they chose to take their families with them."

"Suicide is a helluva thing."

Yvonne's eyes met his. Their piercing-blue held no warmth for the man in front of her. "They had each lost a considerable amount of money prior to their deaths. Some of it through their dealings with you."

"With my company."

"With your company."

"We deal with risk on a daily basis. Granted, some risks are higher than others, but then so are the rewards. Davies and Ball knew the risks but wanted the higher rewards. They lost. It happens sometimes."

"That's a pretty matter-of-fact way of putting it."

"It's a matter-of-fact business. Well, it would be if you didn't go all in."

"Why would experienced businessmen, with families, blow everything?"

"They wanted more. There's nothing wrong with ambition."

"There is when, if you lose, you intend destroying everything you have, including your family...innocent children." The DI could barely hold back her anger, but couldn't give away her suspicion they were murdered. Let him believe she was investigating the deaths as suicides.

One of the two dark-suited guys finally spoke up. "Are you implying that Mr Grantham applied undue pressure on the men to buy risky stock?"

"I'm not implying or assuming anything. I'm merely trying to build a picture. Trying to understand."

"They invested heavily in certain shorts. That's short-term investments, to you." Grantham emphasised the last with a look of disdain, giving Yvonne the distinct impression he didn't like police officers. He continued. "The investments didn't yield as they'd promised. Look, I have to go.

You know, they weren't just dealing with us." He sighed and began to move away, making it clear he felt the interview was over.

"I know. We'll be talking to other companies involved. Would we be able to speak with you again, if needed?"

Mark Grantham tossed a bag over his shoulder. "Sure." He sounded relaxed, but there was a tenseness in his rigid expressions and stiff movements. As soon as he was far enough away, the DI suggested to Dewi that he and Callum should double-check whether Grantham had a criminal record, and look specifically for sexual offences, and to make sure nothing was missed.

LATER THAT EVENING, Tasha pulled up a chair to where Yvonne was seated in the garden. "Penny for them?"

The DI came round from her reverie and smiled thinly at the psychologist. She was feeling world-weary. "Sorry. What time is it?"

"Just after seven." Tasha popped her bag next to the wicker garden chair, into which she plumped herself.

"How was the journey back from London?" Yvonne stood up. "I made some food, and what would you like to drink?"

"I'm okay for a bit. I had a large lunch before I left and a sandwich on the train. Sit for minute and tell me what's going on to make you look so worried. Is it the case you're working?"

"No. We're making progress with it. I've got a lot to tell you. I know you've only been gone a few days but there's been a some significant developments."

"Then what else, Yvonne. I know when something's bothering you."

The DI sighed, placing her chin on her hand. "I talked to my mum the other day. Something I haven't done for some time."

"Are there problems between you two? I have wondered why you don't talk about your parents."

"My father killed himself."

"Oh." Tasha looked at the ground and shook her head. "Yvonne, I'm sorry." Her eyes met the DI's. "You blame your mum?" It was said more like a statement than a question.

Yvonne blinked several times, her eyes glistening. "She had an affair. My father found out and it destroyed him. My mother moved to Australia with the other man."

"Making it hard for you to forgive her and virtually impossible to forgive the other man."

"They moved about three years after my father died."

"Perhaps that was the only way she felt she could continue with her life. Maybe the memories were to painful to stay? How old were you when your father passed away?"

"Mid-teens. I'd just completed GCSEs. One of the last memories I have of my father was at the sea, during the summer holiday, on a camping vacation."

"How were they when they were together, your mum and dad? What was their relationship like?" Tasha sat back in her chair, studying the DI.

Yvonne could feel this turning into a therapy session, something she didn't really want. Still, she answered the question.

"My mother was the life and soul. I'd hear her telling my dad that he took life too seriously. It was she who'd accept the party invites and then persuade my dad it was a good idea. She liked dancing. He liked country walks."

"And, I'm guessing, he wasn't that fond of dancing."

"She'd try to drag him up, at weddings etc, and he'd dig his heels in."

"Hmmmmm."

"But he loved watching her dance. He'd smile with love and pride. I could see how much he adored her."

"How did they meet?"

"They worked for the same company. He was an accountant and she a personal assistant to the boss. Apparently, my dad chased her for ages. He'd wait for her after work, to ask her how her day was. He used to say that he hadn't expected to win her over, but that hadn't stopped him trying." Yvonne smiled. "Romantic don't you think?"

"Very." Tasha rubbed her chin. "But, what you're describing to me is chalk and cheese. You do know that?"

"Of course, they were different, but they had been very much in love."

"Your mum was looking for a more energetic life with your father. As hard as it may be for you to accept, he was struggling to meet her halfway."

"Are you saying the affair was inevitable?"

"Not the affair...the break-up. I think the break-up would have happened at some point, anyway."

"But would my father still have killed himself?"

"How did your mum take his death?"

"She blamed herself. Cried a lot. Self-pity."

"Don't you think you're being a bit tough on her, Yvonne? People sometimes have affairs. They don't expect their partners to end it all."

"She moved away."

"Did you talk to her about it before she moved?"

The DI shook her head. "I couldn't. I couldn't talk to her because I couldn't forgive her."

"Your mum moving away could have more to do with

your rejection of her than her own self-loathing. *And* she probably did blame herself, every bit as much as you blamed her."

"Can I change the subject?"

Tasha pursed her lips. "If you wish?"

Yvonne talked about the case, filling her in regarding the latest developments, but Tasha could see that Yvonne was distracted. The business with her mother wasn't finished, by any means.

RYAN SMITH WAS SAT in the lounge of the 'Willow and Beeches', belonging to Bettws Hall. The lodge was designed to accommodate up to sixteen people in luxury; king-sized, en suite accommodation. Ryan had it all to himself. Lodge staff informed Yvonne and Dewi that this was usually what their more affluent clients required.

The lodge oozed quality, from the locally sourced oak beams to the plush upholstery and accompanying chef and waiting staff. Ryan Smith would want for nothing during his stay. Yvonne was glad of the peaceful atmosphere.

Ryan didn't get up when they entered. He merely raised his head from the paperwork he'd been studying.

He was long and lean, in black jeans and grey t-shirt. His clothes were a perfect fit, hugging obvious muscles.

"Mr Smith I'm..."

"I know who you are, DI Giles. I'm not expecting anyone else."

"This is DS Dewi Hughes." Yvonne thought that introduction probably wasn't needed either, but she wouldn't be silenced - no matter the wealth or the impatience of the interviewee.

"How can I help you, officers?" He said it like he couldn't care less.

"We're exploring the background to the suicides of two local businessmen. I understand both were business clients of yours."

Smith sighed and pushed his paperwork to one side. "Who are we talking about here?"

"Ben Davies, and Tony Ball."

"You mean the guys who killed their families as well as themselves? My company had dealings with them."

"And your company is Highland Finance."

"That's right." He wiped the knee of his jeans free of something non-existent.

"How well did you know them?"

"As well as I know any of my company's clients. I thought they were good at what they did and liked to live life to the full. Their deaths surprised me."

"How did you meet them?"

"They approached me after some of their investments with Boxhall began shrinking."

"I understand you used to work for Boxhall, yourself. Why did you leave?"

The muscles in is face tightened, and he folded his arms. "I suspect you know the answer to that question already."

"I'd like to hear your version." Yvonne's voice was low and soft but the there was an edge to her gaze.

"I was accused of insider trading. I was eventually cleared, but the company let me go. Couldn't afford to have that kind of smell around."

"So you set up your own company..."

"Where's this going?"

A smartly dressed waiter entered after knocking. On sensing the tension, he ducked back out again.

"Please don't feel threatened by us, Mr Smith. We're just filling in some gaps in the backgrounds of the men. Relatives want to know why. You do understand?"

He unfolded his arms. "I don't feel threatened, but neither do I trust the motives of others. You'll forgive me that...given my experience."

Yvonne nodded. "Did you, or anyone in your company, foresee what was going to happen?"

"No."

"Did you think them vulnerable?"

"If you're asking if I preyed on them financially, the answer is no." He got up and walked to the window.

"Did you make a lot of money when they lost money? Or did you lose money, too?"

"You know I don't have to answer that sort of question without a lawyer present."

"Do you think you need a lawyer?"

"That depends on where this is going and what it is you *really* want to know. I am not to blame for their deaths. If that is what you're thinking?"

"I didn't say I was blaming you, Mr Smith."

"They bought into investments with their eyes open."

"I understand Ben Davies had only been an accredited investor for just over a year. Does that really constitute eyes open?"

"They had financial advisers. All investors have financial advisers, independent from fund managers. Maybe you should talk to those guys."

"We will, thank you." Yvonne rose from her seat. "One more thing, Mr Smith, I understand you had a conviction for exposure, aged seventeen. What was that about?"

In that moment, he looked as though she'd punched him. "I took a leak in a park." He spat the words, striding back from the window. "Go. And the next time you want to speak with me, I'll have legal representation."

As they left the lodge, Dewi spoke for the first time since their arrival. "He's nervous about something."

"You think so?" Yvonne surveyed their surroundings. "I think he's hiding something. I don't know if that's related to the deaths, though. He wasn't happy when I mentioned his exposure offence."

"He was a youngster. He could've been taking a leak, like he said."

"People are rarely convicted for just taking a leak, Dewi."

"Fair enough, ma'am."

"I'm curious about his being in the area right now, though: the same time as Mark Grantham. If Ryan Smith left Boxhall Investments under a cloud, what is he doing here at the same time as the Boxhall CEO? *And* both staying in accommodation connected to Bettws Hall."

"I'll look into it, ma'am."

"Thanks, Dewi. We'll get the team together this afternoon for a briefing."

HE USUALLY WATCHED THEM, on and off, for at least six months – dependent on opportunity. The personality of the man was just as important as the look of the woman. The husband had to be a risk-taker. Had to have vulnerabilities to exploit. All he had to do was set things up and patiently watch and wait for the time to be right.

He enjoyed the churning in the depths of his stomach. The shivers. The pins and needles. Every nerve ending tingled. It was always like this when he decided on a new couple. But with every family, he increased the risk of being caught. Paradoxically, this heightened both the pleasure and the fear, evidenced by the pearls of sweat building on his upper lip and soaking his shirt at the base of his spine. His biceps ached from the weight of the binoculars, heavier with every minute he surveyed his quarry.

Thomas Childs left his house for work, unaware of the watcher up on the path. Who had a perfect view of his coastal home. Who watched him get into his Jag and fire up the engine. Who watched the car purr out of sight. Who then turned his attention back to the house. The site of which, was perfect – just around the corner from the Aberystwyth town, along the coastal walk.

Frequented by tourists, he could be anyone, and he had a long view in either direction to ensure he wasn't caught spying. He had to choose his cover carefully but, aside from that, it couldn't be a better location. And, once again, the house had lots and lots of glass.

With the husband gone, he could move in closer. He felt more alive than he had in weeks. He lay down in the sandy grass, binoculars almost flush with the ground. His arms could cope better now.

She moved around the house in her underwear. He couldn't have scripted it better. He checked his watch. Seven-thirty am. He'd have to go soon. The early birds would be out and about with their dogs, or else beginning a hike along the cliff. He wouldn't risk discovery.

16

'Williams and Wells Financial Advisers' had offices in Newtown. Yvonne and Dewi parked as near as they could, without using the public car parks. She could see the river and paused to watch it. The water had been dirtied by recent storms. The turbulence seemed a good metaphor for recent events.

The office's highly polished chrome-and-glass finish was indicative of the wealth of the clients who used the firm, and Yvonne felt as though her mere presence might sully its look. The individuals working there appeared as polished as their surroundings. Not a hair or a piece of clothing out of place. The DI straightened her skirt.

"DI Giles?" A grey-suited, blonde-haired girl directed this at Dewi, who cleared his throat uncomfortably. "? Err...I'm DS Hughes," he said, in a more authoritative tone than he would normally use. "This is DI Giles," he added, holding an arm out towards Yvonne.

The girl smiled at the DI, but without hint of apology. The two detectives followed her towards a suite of rooms off a small corridor. A further young female, in the front office, barely noticed them, typing quickly as she stared at her screen.

Paul Baker rose immediately as they entered. Extending his hand, he waited for them to introduce themselves before confirming who he was.

"Please." He pointed to the comfortable chairs next to his desk. His crisp, metallic-blue suit tossed around the sunlight from the window. His shirt was perfectly ironed.

"I'm sorry to bother you at work." Yvonne took the offered seat, setting her bag next to her feet. Dewi perched on the edge of his chair.

"Well, Darryl okayed it, so it's fine with me. How can I help you?"

Yvonne appreciated his helpful attitude and relaxed a little. "We'll need to speak to Darryl as well. We're trying to tie up some loose ends around the deaths of two businessmen." Once again, Yvonne thought it better to concentrate on the ones in her force area for the time being. "Ben Davies and Tony Ball committed suicide after killing their families. Obviously, that's left their wider families and friends with a lot of questions they'd like answered."

"Yes." Paul stared through the window, his face grave. There was a second or two of silence before he continued. "I knew both men, of course." He raised his head to look the DI directly in the eyes. "What would you like to know?"

"I understand you're a junior partner in the company."

"Yes, that's right. Though I wouldn't say I did the junior share of the work."

"How much time did you spend with either of the men?"

"Errrm...well, I spoke with them probably once a month, on an official basis."

"Did you ever see them unofficially?"

"Occasionally socialised with them. Darryl knew them

better than I. He arranged for me to go with him to a party Ben Davies was holding a couple of years back. I continued to go to the odd social gathering, from that point really."

"You knew his family?"

"I did. Lovely family. It's senseless, a senseless waste."

"Did you have any idea that something like this could happen? Were the family unhappy?"

"Ben lost a lot of money. His financial dealings didn't work out the way he planned. We introduced him to the firms he invested with. After that, he would do his own thing and just check in with us now and again. We warned him a few times about the risks he was taking. His head did go down towards the end."

"Did he get on with his wife?"

"He always seemed happy to me...until the end, like I said."

"What about Tony Ball?"

"Tony could be stern. I'd seen him lose his patience with Darryl a few times?"

"You mean Darryl your senior partner?"

"Yes, I think Tony partly blamed Darryl for the mess he got into. He'd gone to him for some advice on trades and investments he was considering. He accepted the advice and wasn't happy with the result. Darryl saw more of Tony than I did. He could tell you more about that."

"How often did you socialise with Tony and his family?" It was Dewi's turn to ask a few questions.

"Well, again, I went to a few parties. Garden parties in the summer, mostly." Paul Baker ran his hand through his short, dark, hair. "Once or twice, I went to a country do when both men were in attendance."

"They knew each other, then?"

"In passing, so to speak. I don't think they were big friends or anything."

"Did you see what was coming for either man and their families?"

"Absolutely not."

The grey-suited blonde assistant was back. Her heels click-clacked on the parquet flooring. "Mr Williams will see you now."

Yvonne and Dewi rose obediently. The DI gave a small wave to Baker as she left his room.

Darryl Williams, Senior Financial Adviser, took off his reading glasses and sat back in his chair. It was clear from his expression that he expected them to introduce themselves, and Yvonne did exactly that.

He indicated the chairs on the other side of his imposing Victorian desk. Yvonne had the urge to stay standing but thought better of it. Dewi pulled his chair out, scraping it noisily over the floor. The DI felt a perverse pleasure at this, and the pained wince from Williams.

Although in his early fifties, he appeared lean, and the broad shoulders gave the appearance of a strong man. His tweed jacket looked a little dated, with its brown leather elbow patches. Yvonne wondered if he wore it deliberately, to convey a certain image.

He raised one eyebrow and the DI cleared her throat. "DI Giles, Dyfed-Powys Police." As she took out her notebook, she felt like she was arming herself.

Dewi's voice was once more uncharacteristically stern. "DS Hughes."

"Darryl Williams, Senior Adviser and CEO of this firm. How can I help, officers?" He said it between clenched teeth, whilst managing to look bored.

"We're investigating the suicides of two local businessmen. We understand they were patrons of your firm."

He shifted to a more upright position, his eyes searching the DI's face. "Investigating suicides? I don't understand. Investigating, why?"

"We'd like to tie up loose ends regarding the circumstances of the deaths and give closure to the families." Yvonne did some facial searching of her own.

"Are you aware of the gentlemen we're referring to?" Dewi flicked through a couple of pages of his notebook.

"Well, I would think that Ben Davies would be one and..." He paused, screwing up his eyes as though struggling to recall another name. The DI didn't believe the charade, but helped him out anyway. "Tony Ball."

"Ahhh, yes...Tony."

"How well did you know him?"

"I only knew him on a business footing, really. I'd known him for about ten years."

"What about socially?" Yvonne was still scrutinising Darryl's face.

"Not really."

"Are you saying you have never attended social events with him?"

There was a pause. Darryl squeezed his bottom lip with his teeth.

"I might have. We sometimes have business conferences and business events which are social in nature."

It was clear he wasn't intending to be helpful. The rest of the interview wasn't any better. Afterward, Yvonne rose to thank him for his time, but her displeasure must have shown on her face, as Darryl rose to shake her hand before they left.

"I'm sorry, inspector, I probably haven't been much help."

THE DI HAD FELT her blood pressure rising, and she barely waited until she was outside of the offices. "If he'd been any cagier he could have housed the animals in Chester Zoo!" She blurted the words, her fists clenched.

Dewi couldn't help a smile curling his lips. He had seen during the interview that she was controlling her irritation, which increased by the minute. "I think he's hiding something, ma'am. And did you notice the masonic ring?"

"I noticed the ring, Dewi. So, it was masonic?"

"Looked like it to me. There's a lodge on Milford Road. Maybe we could go along there at some point and make enquiries. May be an interesting list of members."

"What if they were all in it together?" Yvonne turned to face her DS. "What if there's some kind of conspiracy here to defraud wealthy businessmen out of their estate and they're all involved?"

"You mean a cover-up?"

"Or an organised criminal network..."

"I don't think it's likely, if I'm honest, but stranger things have happened, I guess. The world of business is a magical mystery to me."

"Well done, spotting the mason's ring, Dewi. We'll certainly do some digging there. I need a chat with Llewellyn." Yvonne began crossing the road and narrowly missed being hit by a cyclist. She pulled back just in time.

"What are you going to say to the DCI? Are you going to talk to him about Darryl Williams?"

"No, I want to talk to him about bringing Tasha on board, officially."

"You do know you're risking another budget argument..." Dewi gave a chuckle.

"Well, she's offered to do it *pro bono* if necessary. I'm providing bed and board." Yvonne grinned. "Come on, it's lunchtime, and I don't know about you, but I'm starving."

YVONNE LISTENED at the door before giving it a couple of firm knocks.

"Come in." The reply was slow and the voice cracked.

"Hi., is this a bad time?" Yvonne walked in as though afraid of waking someone.

"No, why do you ask?"

"You sound tired and..." She eyed the messed up paperwork on his desk.

He ran his hands through his hair and sighed. Sitting back in his chair, his face relaxed a little. "Just a headache." He managed a weak smile. "What can I do for you?"

"I feel like I'm making headway with this case, but I'm still a way off having a concrete suspect." She brushed her hand on her skirt. "There are people of interest," she added quickly.

He indicated for her to take a seat, and pulled his own chair around to the same side of the desk. "Have you a definite link between the rapes?"

Yvonne's gaze strayed to the window. It was drizzling outside. The sky had darkened considerably in the last hour, though it was the middle of the day. She watched the rivulets form, fuse, and fade as they journeyed down the pane. "I have. I'd say there is now very little doubt we have a serial rapist operating in the area."

"Well, that's something, at least."

Yvonne nodded. "What I was going to ask was if I might bring in extra help."

The DCI frowned. "Help?"

Yvonne grimaced, as though afraid of the answer she might get. "I was wondering if I might bring in Tasha Phillips." She finished the sentence quickly and sat back in her chair, as though exhausted by the effort it took to ask the question.

"Yvonne, as much as I respect and admire your psychologist friend, we can't make a habit of drawing her in for every investigation. The police and crime commissioner have been hammering the chief super about our budget for some time. Right now, we're having to invest in recruitment. You know we're going to have to shut Newtown reception one day a week due to uniform shortage. Not enough bodies to man the station."

Yvonne nodded. "I had heard. I was hoping it wouldn't come to that."

"Well, it has." He moved his head a little too quickly and winced.

"Have you taken some pain killers?"

"Not yet, I was hoping I might shake it without them."

Yvonne took a couple of paracetamol from the box in her jacket pocket.

"You got a headache, too?" He asked, accepting them from her.

"I did have. I think it's the closeness of this weather. I think a storm's coming."

It was his turn to gaze through the window. "Yes, you may be right...in more ways than one," he added.

"She's offered to do it for free."

"Sorry?"

"Tasha. She's offered to help us on the case for free. And

I'd value her input on my investigation into the family deaths."

"She'd seriously do it for free? That's quite a friend..."

"Well, I said she could have free bed and board at my place. So, kind of like a working holiday."

Llewellyn laughed. "Okay. Okay. Bring her on board. I'll ask the super if there's any money for her."

"Great." Yvonne smiled warmly and appeared much younger.

"When was she planning to come down?"

"Err..." Yvonne cringed.

Llewellyn laughed again, shaking his head. "I might have known. What if I'd said no?" He held up his hand. "Don't tell me, I think I know the answer. Just remember, I want to know ev-er-y-thing." He emphasised the syllables to ram home the message. "You two, together, spells trouble."

Yvonne smiled with real warmth as she left his office.

BRIAN EVANS SAT with a duty solicitor in interview room one. DC Callum Jones waited with them for the DI to arrive. When she did, he began the introductions for the benefit of the tape. She gave her name and rank on cue.

It was evident from their faces they were very unhappy about being called into the station at seven o'clock in the morning. They had a sullen schoolboy look about them.

"Mr Evans, thank you for coming here today to be interviewed in connection with an alleged sexual assault which took place in Welshpool on the twenty-second of July."

"What assault? I haven't assaulted anyone."

"We're not accusing you, Mr Evans. We're merely making enquiries, and we do have good reasons for asking you to come."

"My client would like you to put forward those reasons at the outset." The solicitor glared at Yvonne, over the top of his glasses, as he shuffled through paperwork in front of him.

Yvonne ran her pen over her notes as she began. "First of all, the method of the attack was similar to an assault which Mr Evans perpetrated two years ago."

"My client has completed a treatment programme. He's doing well on his licence. I have a glowing report from his-"

"Secondly, there was an absence period from his electronic tag on the night in question for an hour." Yvonne leaned back in her chair, placing her pen down. "What does your client have to say about that?"

"I had a good reason for that absence." Evans gave the DI a black look.

"It says here you were breached for that absence and narrowly escaped recall to prison."

From the way the solicitor stared at his client it was clear he hadn't been given that information. Evans chewed his fingernails.

"Where were you that night, Mr Evans?"

"I needed more weed. I went to see my friend, who's also my supplier, and we started smoking together. I lost track of time."

"You know you could be recalled to prison for using cannabis."

"I didn't assault anyone." Evans scowled at the DI.

Yvonne noted the yellow staining on Evans' fingers; the hair straggled and matted; days worth of stubble on his face and clothing mottled by food stains. Evans appeared as though he hadn't had a bath in weeks.

"Do you have running water where you are? And electricity?"

Callum looked at her.

"What do you mean?" Evans looked surprised. "Of course I do."

"Are you okay financially?"

"I'm getting by."

"Do you have a support worker?"

"Just my probation officer."

"Uh huh."

"What's this about?" Evans had gone back to sullen.

Yvonne pushed her chair back in a staccato movement, her mind suddenly elsewhere. "Thank you for talking to us, Mr Evans. We'll be in touch if we need to speak to you again."

CALLUM STOPPED her in the corridor after Evans and his solicitor had left. "I don't understand, ma'am. That was a bit short and sweet. Are you taking it on face value, what he said about smoking with his dealer?"

"Did you take a good look at him, Callum? There's no way he could be described as smelling of expensive soap, or any soap."

Callum grinned. "Okay, I'm with you on that."

"Talk to his probation officer anyway. Get her take on the absence. See if there have been other absences from curfew. Any that haven't been followed up with breach. If there have been others, compare them with the dates and times of the other assaults."

"Yes, ma'am."

"I doubt he's our guy. There's a part of me that feels sorry for him. He really doesn't have much, does he? But, I don't want to leave any stone unturned in this investigation."

"I'm on it like a car bonnet."

Yvonne chuckled, raising an eyebrow. "You got that from your kids?"

Callum smiled. "They keep me young."

GOING HOME THAT EVENING, Yvonne couldn't wait to let Tasha know that she might be officially part of the investigation. She felt more optimism than she had in a while.

17

There was a coldness to the clear morning air and a light breeze tugged at the tops of the trees. It was only mid-August, and yet Yvonne was reminded of Autumn.

They'd left the car a hundred yards down the lane, making a conscious effort to approach the house as they imagined a killer would have done. Tasha walked ahead, followed closely by Yvonne and Dave West, the DC from West Mercia.

From the outside, there was little to indicate that anything dark had happened there. The birds still sang and flew from hedgerow to hedgerow. The countryside was fresh, green and peaceful. The approach to the house was pretty ordinary, devoid of police tape. The blinds were closed on most of the downstairs windows and a 'For Sale' sign loomed large on the main wrought-iron gates. The latter were not locked.

"A killer would probably have parked where we did." Tasha paused outside the front door. "It's the only place with enough foliage around to provide cover. Only someone visiting the house would see it."

"He'd be taking a risk with that though, wouldn't he?"

"Ordinarily, yes, but bear in mind that they were killed somewhere between midnight and the small hours. Who's going to turn up at that time? Unless they also have bad business in mind. He'd have been unlucky for someone else to just happen upon them."

Yvonne nodded. "Shall we go in?" She took the keys, with their estate-agent-supplied key fob, and opened the front door. Their footsteps echoed around the large spaces, now devoid of furniture and possessions. The DI could imagine only too well the footfall, shouts and laughter of those small children, as they drove their mum and dad to distraction. That was just a few short weeks ago.

She leaned back on a wall and sighed. There was nothing now. Even the carpets were absent. They trod on ash and oak flooring, or else on clay tiles. Otherwise, all indicators of the lives of the family, were gone.

Dave West opened his file containing the crime-scene photographs, which the DI had given back to him in the car. She no longer needed them. The images were all-too-readily called to mind and she could see the dead, clearly, as she entered each room.

Off the hall, they entered the largest of the open-plan spaces. A huge kitchen diner, filled with light, once Tasha pressed the remote button to open the blinds. At the far end of the space had been a massive corner suite, where the family might have relaxed, played and fought as Mrs Bennett prepared dinner. Had a killer watched them through those large windows?

The kitchen was where Mr Bennett had lost his life. The

air was filled with the lingering odour of fresh paint. The flooring had been sanded and waxed.

The bedrooms, too, had been painted. The window in the master bedroom, left partially open.

"The Bennett's bed was here." Yvonne indicated its position, verified by Dave as he oriented the photo in his hand.

"She'd woken up prior to being killed. She may even have been walking around. We have no way of knowing." Dave pointed to the spot. "A book had been dropped on the floor just there, close to the door."

"You think Mrs Bennett dropped it? Maybe when the killer came to the bedroom door?" Tasha walked over to where Dave and Yvonne were standing.

"I do. I think she heard something, got out of bed to check it out, and came face to face with killer and the gun."

"So, she may have been awake and reading, and been fully aware of the gunshot that took her husband's life."

"That's what I think." Dave pursed his lips. "Shaun, that's my DS, thought it had probably been discarded previously, or knocked there by the children. There were a few items here and there, in the downstairs rooms, too. The book was open, face-down, and the some of the pages were creased."

Yvonne took a step back. "So, Mr Bennett is killed down in the kitchen-diner. Mrs Bennett hears the bang and walks to the door, to investigate, carrying the book. The killer is on the landing, he aims the gun at her – ordering her back into the room - then he shoots her."

"Yes." Dave nodded. "We don't know exactly how it transpired, but we do know that Mrs Bennett was not under the covers when she was shot. Her body was moved there and covered up *after* the event. In fact, judging by the amount of blood around, we think the killer went to the children's room and dispatched them before coming back to tuck Mrs Bennett in."

"And there were no signs of sexual assault." Yvonne walked to the window, watching the trees shudder in the light breeze.

"There was no evidence of any sexual activity that night, forced or otherwise."

"I have a thought." Tasha joined the DI at the bedroom window.

"What's that?" Yvonne turned to her.

"When looking at the other families, we assumed that the mothers were asleep when they were killed, as they had been shot in bed. Stands to reason that a loving husband would wait for them to be asleep. But an outsider? He may have ordered them to do other stuff before sending them back into bed and shooting them."

"That's right." Yvonne nodded, and a shiver ran down her spine. "We'll never know what actually took place. Not unless the killer confesses everything."

"And how often do they do that?" Tasha sighed.

"Quite, the memories of those last moments are something they can still have control over, when all else has been taken from them."?

"'Til they write a book..." Dave West threw the words behind him. He was already making his way to the children's rooms.

"Again, there's no evidence that the children knew anything about it," he said as the others joined him.

"Wouldn't they have been woken by the noise from the mother's room?"

Dave shrugged. "If they were, there was no sign of that from the scene."

"You said that the scene was organised, and neat."

"It was. Particularly the children's room. Something just didn't feel right about it."

"What about the book in the Master bedroom?"

"That was the exception."

"An organised killer would have tidied that up, surely." Yvonne leaned back against the wall, pulling forward again to check the back of her jacket when she remembered that the place had recently been painted.

Tasha rubbed her chin. "If our killer is a sexual predator, as I suspect he is, the mother's room is where he would be most likely to make a mistake. It's the room where he's feels most stimulated."

Yvonne nodded. "Seeing his quarry in the flesh, so-to-speak."

"*And* this was his first crime scene. Again, a place where he'd be most likely to make an error," Tasha added.

"Was there anything else that stood out for you?" Yvonne asked the question of Dave.

"Only the children's teddies, all neatly lined up on the shelves, along with their tiny blankets. I've got small children. They've got all sorts on their beds, and in them, when I tuck them up at night."

Yvonne nodded. "Why did he take them away? That is the question. Why remove them from sleeping children, before killing them?"

HE'D BROUGHT NIGHT-VISION BINOCULARS, as the night was dark and moonless. If anyone approached along the coastal path he'd see them long before they saw him.

Thomas Childs was out again, on a late-night business function. He wouldn't be back any time soon. Marion Childs was alone, downstairs. The children, Christian and Margot, were asleep in bed.

He watched her potter around her kitchen, a half-finished glass of wine on the counter-top. That was her second. She was probably feeling quite relaxed and a little less aware of her surroundings. He felt safe, out here in the darkness, with enough distance between himself and the house for him to need binoculars.

He heard a sound off to his left and scanned the horizon with his naked eyes. Seeing nothing, he took a look through his night-vision glasses – heart thumping. A dog. He hoped it didn't come over. Seeing it head back off in the other direction, he turned his attention back to the house.

Mrs Childs must be listening to music. She'd picked her wine glass up again and was swaying to and fro. This was more like it. He'd wait an hour or more sometimes just for moments like these. It was another tortuously humid night. Marion Childs had tied her hair back in a ponytail. He imagined the sweat beading on her upper lip, as he watched her brush her fringe back, as though to cool down her forehead. It was almost too much. He felt the stirring in his trousers but chose to do nothing about it. Sometimes it was good just to suffer the tease.

He liked the dress she was wearing. Flowery and sleeveless. There was an innocence about her. He liked that. The second glass of wine was now almost gone. His heart skipped a beat as she turned fully to the window, still swaying. It seemed like she was looking straight at him, though he knew she was not.

She made a rapid turn, moving swiftly to the island. Her mobile phone must be going off. She put it to her ear, sitting down on a bar stool – her back to him.

Distant voices shook him from his reverie and he put his

night vision to his face once more. Youngsters. Students, probably. He began his retreat in the other direction, sure that they could not see him. Even if they could, he knew they wouldn't be able to see him clearly. That was the trouble with a university town. Students got everywhere.

18

Yvonne had her wellies on. Dewi was still in his shoes. He pulled a face at her when they became covered in mud from an unexpected puddle, the other side of a stile they had just climbed over.

The DI let out a giggle. "Oops, I did warn you."

"Yeah, thanks." Dewi's feigned impatience made her laugh again. She stopped laughing, however, as they approached the group in country tweeds, caps and waterproof jackets – the expensive kind.

Intermittent shots rang out and hurt her ears a little more, the closer they got. One of the group spotted them and tapped the others on the shoulder, one of them mid-aim. The shot rang out and the clay pigeon carried on spinning to the ground, intact.

"You were expecting us?" Yvonne directed this at the shoot organiser, Evan Morris. She flashed her ID around the group, taking a perverse pleasure from the act.

She'd spoken to Evan the day before, about attending one of his summer shoots. She just hadn't told him when. This was the shoot she knew Mark Grantham would be attending. What she hadn't known, and what took her aback right now, was that Ryan Smith would also be attending. Two prominent CEOs in the same field. Given what she knew of their history, she hadn't expected them to be sharing the same air.

"Are you following me, Inspector?" Mark Grantham put the gun over his arm and walked forward, standing over her. It was times like this she wished she were a few inches taller.

"I hadn't thought of it like that." She cocked her head to one side. "But now you come to mention it."

He put one hand on the folded shotgun. "It can be dangerous walking onto a field when men are shooting."

It felt like a threat. Yvonne opened her notebook and took a step forward, into his personal space. "Is that a masonic ring you're wearing?"

Grantham took a step back, handing his gun to a guy who was obviously an aide of some kind. "You want to speak to me?" He said the words with a force which betrayed his anger, only just held in check.

"Yes, my DS would like to speak with Mr Smith." She turned to Ryan Smith, who reluctantly handed his gun over to the aide and walked towards Dewi.

"Will this take long? Only, we've got lunch organised, and I've got a business meeting this afternoon." Ryan rubbed his gun shoulder.

Yvonne turned to Smith. "Business? I thought this was leisure-time for you."

"I can combine both," he stated, calmly.

"Oh come on, let's do it. Then these *plods* can be on their merry way." Grantham gave the DI a sneer which dared her to answer back. She bit her lip. He tipped his cap back on his head. "Go on then, officer." He said, as they separated off from the others. "What you investigating now? Any kittens run over in the area, have they? Or has someone scratched the paint on someone's car? Sorry not me, I wasn't there."

"Most people have a helpful attitude towards the police, Mr Grantham."

"I'm not most people. And yes, the ring is masonic."

"Are you a member of a lodge?"

"I am. What's that got to do with anything?"

"Just showing interest, Mr Grantham."

"I've never known the police ask a question just because they were interested. Look, I'm a very busy man. If you've got something to ask me, or even a reason to be here, then give it to me straight. Don't pussy-foot around me. I can't stand time wasters."

The DI bit her lip again. This man really was obnoxious. "Have you ever been to Maesbury?"

"Maesbury?"

"Maesbury March."

"No idea where that is." He said the words as though they were bits of dirt, to be flicked off his jacket. "Why do you ask?"

"What about Montgomery? Or Welshpool?"

"Montgomery? Yes, I've been there. I've been there on my own and I've taken my team there on team-building weekends. Why?"

"A female from Montgomery was raped in Welshpool three weeks ago. She described a man who could have been you – tweed cap, smartly dressed, waterproof jacket - who had shown an interest in her in Montgomery."

"Half the other men in this field, and in many other fields around the country, are dressed just like that." He stated the last loudly, inviting laughter from the other men.

Dewi looked over from where he was interviewing Ryan Smith, some hundred yards away.

"The victim stated that the suspect announced he was into money."

"What on earth..."

"You were in the area at the time."

"And that's it? What kind of evidence is that?"

"I came to ask if you'd attend a line-up."

"You don't like me, do you?" He sneered at her. His face tense. Teeth clenched. "This is persecution. Harassment. My lawyers will be all over you like a rash. By the time they've finished with you, your career will be shredded." His eyes spat venom at her.

"Fill your boots." Yvonne gazed steadily back at him. "I'd still like you to attend a line-up."

"Is that all?" He made as though to turn away from her.

"You're still on friendly terms with Ryan Smith, then?"

"Why wouldn't I be?" His voice was filled with exasperation.

"I understand he left your company under a cloud."

"I see you've done your research."

"It's what I'm paid to do."

"Well, you're chasing the wrong guy."

"I'll be the judge of that."

He turned on his heel and strode away. She didn't attempt to stop him. She'd finished with him. For now.

Dewi joined her soon after.

"How did it go, ma'am?"

"Not great... How about you?"

"Smith was wearing a mason's ring, too."

"I think they all were."

"Could be significant?"

"Maybe, I don't think we should get hung up on it, though. Masons do some good work. Charitable work."

"They also help cover for each other." Dewi shook his soggy feet.

"Yes, perhaps." It was just approaching lunchtime and Yvonne was already tired.

As they crossed the field, back towards the stile, the shooting began again. The first shot made the DI jump. Heart pounding, she walked a little faster away from the men and their guns.

It was only once they were back at their car that they exchanged thoughts about the two men they'd just interviewed.

Ryan Smith had given Dewi a hard time, but he could see from her face that the DI had probably had the worst of it. He felt outrage at the open threat issued by Grantham. Smith had fallen short of such a gesture, but denied ever being in either Maesbury March or Montgomery. Both men had been wearing far too many clothes for either Dewi or Yvonne to know if they smelled of expensive soap.

BACK AT BASE CAMP, DC Clayton greeted them at the door. "Morning, ma'am. The DCI has asked that you go see him in his office as soon as you can."

Yvonne looked at Dewi with raised eyebrows before looking back at Clayton and thanking him for the info. She headed to Llewellyn's office immediately, breathing deeply before knocking hard.

"Come in." He sounded unusually stern. She rubbed her hands down her skirt, straightened her hair, and pushed open the door.

"You wanted to see me, sir?"

"I've had the superintendent on the phone, not ten minutes ago. He's not happy."

"Oh? Why's that?"

"The Police and Crime Commissioner has been bending his ear about your harassment of a prominent CEO. Care to enlighten me?"

Yvonne sighed and rolled her eyes. "Oh god, I'm sorry. I can explain."

"I think you'd better."

"I've asked Mark Grantham, CEO of Boxhall Investments, to come in for a line-up. I'll be asking the sexual assault victims to pick out their attacker."

"What makes you think it might be him?"

"Appearance, opportunity, and the money connection. Plus he did an endorsement last year of a brand of soap containing sandalwood." Yvonne hoped the information she'd gotten from Tasha, the evening before, would clinch it. Tasha was still helping with social media research, and the sandalwood soap adverts had gotten her very excited.

Llewellyn studied her face for a few moments. "Okay, I'll back you," he said, finally. "But the PCC is not a happy woman, and if he passes the line-up, I want you to leave the man alone. At least until you have hard evidence to back up an intervention."

"He's trying to influence my investigation. Don't you find that a little suspicious?"

"He's also a very busy man, and busy men don't have a lot of patience. People like that hate delays or unexpected users of their time. Their impatience spills over into complaints. Especially against police officers."

"He's pretty high on my list of suspects."

"Promise you'll leave him alone for a while, if he isn't picked out of the line-up."

"I will, sir." Yvonne headed for the door, turning just before she reached it. "Just for a while."

SHE HEADED in search of Dewi, and found him munching on a tuna sandwich.

"So, what did you make of Ryan Smith?"

"Cagey, very cagey. He denies being in the area at the time of the sexual assault on Tina Pugh."

"Hmmm, anything else?"

"He kept looking over at Grantham, or you, or both."

"Nervous?"

"Hard to say. The man's a closed book. Like he's well-practised at hiding things from people."

"Interesting, I think those two men are knee-deep in something. I have no idea what, yet. But definitely in cahoots."

"Smith wears a masonic ring, too."

"I'm organising a line-up for Tina and the other women to take a look at our CEOs. I'm not going to be popular, but I want both Grantham and Smith in that line-up."

"You afraid there might be red tape?"

"I've already had the DCI on my back. Grantham is going to make this as difficult for us as he can. Perversely, that just makes me all the more determined to get to the bottom of their business dealings."

"Want me to get onto fraud squad at the Met?"

"Please."

"Will do."

TASHA DROVE whilst Yvonne flicked through notes and jotted down her ideas. It was a hot, beautiful, sticky day with just enough cloud to cast intriguing shadows around the mid-morning landscape.

The plan was to park the car in Montgomery main square and hike up to the castle. Tasha had a feeling a killer might have used the ruins as a place to watch the Balls' house. The idea was to follow in his footsteps again, looking for the most likely place from which he might have stalked them. He may have left something there.

The walk was steep but engaging, filled with the sweet heady scents of summer. Jasmine and honeysuckle. However, halfway up the winding road, negotiating the craggy outcrop, they began to regret the decision to walk. The humidity sapped their energy and one bottle of water was already gone.

The sight of the walkway to the castle, over the long wooden bridge, filled them with relief. They paused on the bridge to look down at what would have been the castle moat. It was now only a dry indentation, with large rocks and boulders here and there along its length.

As they continued along the slatted bridge, Yvonne wondered if they really were walking in the footsteps of a killer-stalker, and a shiver ran down her back. This shiver returned, intensifying, as they reached what was left of the castle gates and she read the heritage board, put their by Cadw. The story was of the woman in red - Maud Vras – who, on the first of January in twelve eighty-eight, was murdered in the gatehouse by a rock thrown down onto her head. Apparently, Maud had gone there to reclaim a saucepan she'd lent to William of St. Albans, the deputy constable to the Castle. The jury believed William when he claimed that his robe had dislodged the rock by accident. Yvonne tutted to herself.

"Want to share? " Tasha came over to look at the board and Yvonne gave her the gist of the story.

Tasha put her hands in her pockets. "Didn't have you on the case, did they," she laughed.

Yvonne didn't answer, she was still visualising the crumpled body of the woman in red.

Once in the castle's inner ward, the views from the castle became apparent and were breathtaking. There was enough left of the walls and towers to give a good idea of how the castle must once have been. The ruin walls were low enough that anyone standing at them had an astonishingly uninterrupted view of the valley and the picturesque Shropshire hills beyond. More importantly, their killer could have used this place as stalking point. A pair of binoculars would have given him an extremely good view of the Balls' house.

"Here, I think he would have stood here." Tasha leaned on the rocky wall and made as though to hold binoculars to her eyes. Yvonne took a small pair from her bag and they took it in turns to view the house.

"You can clearly see into virtually every window at the back of the house." Tasha handed the binoculars back to Yvonne.

"That's right, all except Tony Ball's study which is hidden by the tree."

Yvonne was looking for something – anything – that the killer might have left up here, but saw nothing. "Someone must come up here cleaning around," she said ruefully.

"I think the Cadw Trust would make sure the ruins remain pristine. If your killer did come up here, whatever he might have left would have long been taken away." Tasha stepped back from the wall. "You were saying that Mark Grantham reported you for harrassing him."

Yvonne sat down on the grass. "He did. I've really rattled him. We're doing a line-up in a couple of days. Both he and Ryan Smith are in the area and will be viewed by the rape victims."

"Nervous?"

"Yes, but hopeful, I get the impression Mark Grantham is as slippery as they come. He's also controlling. Well, he's not going to control the direction of my investigation."

"Hmmm, what's he got to hide?"

"Exactly."

They continued their walk down around the outside of the castle walls, following the route the moat would have taken. There was no-one else around, but it was clear that anyone up here would be able to hear and see the approach of the others and, if necessary, beat a hasty retreat. The perfect place for a watcher.

"I doubt your killer will turn out to be Mark Grantham." Tasha took another bottle of water from her bag and took a long swig, handing it to the DI.

"I get that he's a busy CEO, Tasha, but he's regularly in the area, has his own aircraft, and is *very* chummy with the airport staff at Welshpool."

"I'm not saying he hasn't got something to hide, regarding the financial losses of the victims, but he's not local. Your stalker chap would be given confidence by knowing the area thoroughly. He'll be from these parts and, I suspect, live not too far from here. Whoever he is, he *will* have time on his hands. Time to kill...if you pardon the pun. More time than your Mark Grantham is likely to have."

"Unless he has a deputy he can entrust the business to, whenever he needs to."

"Well, that should be easy enough to check. If his company was investigated by the Met, they'll have that sort of info."

"Good thinking, I knew I brought you on board for something." Yvonne laughed and took another swig from Tasha's bottle.

Neither of them noticed the solitary coke can lying beneath the hedgerow.

19

Two days later, and Yvonne and Dewi nervously awaited the three victims of the serial rapist. There would be six men involved in the line-up, including both Mark Grantham and Ryan Smith. They would be dressed in dark clothing and a mask similar to that worn by the attacker in each of the rapes.

All of similar height and build. The men wouldn't be brought in until the women felt they were ready. The victim and family liaison officers would be responsible for helping the victims relax as much as possible. Yvonne and Dewi would be giving the line-up participants their instructions through the microphone.

Angela Barnes from Maesbury was the first to arrive, accompanied by her parents. Once seated, they spoke in hushed tones. Angela held her mother's hand and leaned her head on her father's shoulder. Something she may not have done since she was a girl, the DI mused.

Tina Pugh and Sarah Evans arrived almost together, and were immediately taken to separate parts of the waiting area. Officers made them cups of tea and prepared them for what was to come. With all victims now present, Yvonne began to relax just a little. One of her biggest fears had been a victim no-show.

She admired the courage of the three women before her. She could see the comfort they were finding in seeing others like themselves. Others who had known the fear and pain and even self-recrimination, so undeserved. The fear that doing the ordinary every day, or having fun, as young women should, had put them at risk. That they had put themselves at risk. She could see it in their faces. Even now, they partly blamed themselves. Yvonne's heart went out to them.

Callum tapped her on the shoulder and drew her to one side. "Grantham has arrived, ma'am. He's kicking off and demanding the line-up be held straight away."

"Thanks, Callum." Yvonne followed her DC out of the room and down the corridor, to where Grantham had been taken and offered coffee.

"Mr. Grantham." Yvonne felt an uncomfortable pleasure in having this arrogant man wait. Uncomfortable because she didn't usually believe in causing others discomfort and Grantham was, as yet, only a suspect. He'd probably hurt a few people in his time, though. If not physically, then emotionally. "I hear you're in a hurry."

"Well, how long is this going to take. My time costs." He ran his hands through his hair, his eyes narrow and accusing.

"You'll understand the need to settle the victims. Their comfort is our priority. They've already been through a lot." Yvonne met his steely glare with one of her own. "We will, of course, keep you waiting only as long as is necessary. Is their anything else my officers can get you?"

"No."

"Have you had the procedure explained to you?"

He scowled at her. "Yes."

"Then I'll leave you to drink your coffee and then you'll be instructed further."

With that, she left him to it. She couldn't help the half-smile which curled her lips. She hoped he hadn't seen it. Something about him made her stomach churn. She felt some fear at having this man as her enemy.

Thirty minutes later and the girls were ready. They sat in a row, watching the room behind the large window, as though about to watch a movie, except each had a visible tremble to their hands, when they raised their cups to their mouths. Yvonne's own heart raced. This was a big deal.

The men filed in. The DI knew immediately which one was Grantham. He was number two. She was having a hard time picking out Ryan Smith. He was either number three or six. She drew in a deep breath.

Each of the men stepped forward when shouted by number, saying, "I do money. *You* wouldn't know what that is." They then had to grunt several times. Yvonne was taken aback at the words when spoken by Mark Grantham. He sounded relaxed. Casual, not the impatient, driven man she'd spoken to only thirty minutes before. He could almost have been someone else. She kept her face passive for fear of giving her feelings away to the witnesses.

There were other phrases for the men, following that. Words relevant to Angela and Sarah. Again, the DI was struck by how casual Mark Grantham was.

Ryan Smith was number six. She recognised him when he spoke. He sounded hoarse, however, like he was recovering from a bad cold.

The men were then led away, only to reappear several

minutes later wearing flat caps and wax jackets. They repeated the 'money' phrase.

Each of the witnesses were then taken to separate rooms and asked if they had seen their attacker in the line. The conversations were recorded for evidence.

Tina Pugh shook her head. "I don't think he was there. I didn't recognise any of the men." Sarah Evans tentatively picked out number four – PC Davies. Angela Barnes broke down. "I'm sorry, I don't know."

"It's okay." Yvonne's gaze and voice was gentle. "I can't thank you enough for coming here today. We'll find the man who hurt you. Today just wasn't the day, but we will."

20

Yvonne's head was in her hands, when Dewi brought her a fresh coffee.

"Hey, come on, this was a long-shot anyway, remember?"

"I know, Dewi. We're just no further forward. And it's not just about preventing another rape. It's about preventing another family from being murdered. I know it. I just know."

"You know we're going to have to leave Mark Grantham and Ryan Smith alone, now..."

"I know." Yvonne sighed. "Well, if they're innocent, it's right that we do. I feel...I feel..."

"Deflated?" Dewi set the coffee down on the desk next to her.

"I got carried away. I let personal dislike get the better of me."

"Well, not one of the victims was absolutely sure of anything. We still cannot completely rule out either Grantham or Smith. We just can't go after them at the moment."

Yvonne pushed her chair back. "Let's get the client list

from Williams and Wells. And if we can't get that, let's at least get the files they hold on the dead men. See exactly what information the firm had."

"Right you are, ma'am."

TASHA WAS LEAVING the DCI's office, as Yvonne headed back to CID, and she was smiling. "Officially on board now." She winked at the DI.

Yvonne gave a weak smile in return. "What did he say?"

"Are you all right?" Tasha put a hand on the DI's shouder.

"The victims failed to pick out anyone from the line-up. That includes Mark Grantham and Ryan Smith."

"Oh..."

"Yeah, thrown me a bit. What did Chris say? Is he going to pay you?"

"He didn't mention fees. He asked me if I'd completed a profile for the rapist. I told him I'd prepared two."

"Hey, I haven't seen a profile, yet. And you've done two?"

"Yes, one is a rapist, who isn't killing. The other, a rapist who has also murdered three families."

"Okay, so what are we looking at?"

"Have lunch with me and I'll tell you." Tasha's cheeky grin was irresistible and the DI laughed. "Holding the police to ransom, eh?"

"If I have to?"

"I'll get my bag."

THEY DECIDED ON 'LA TERRAZA', the little Italian restaurant in Park Street, not far from the station. They asked for somewhere quiet and the waiter showed them to a tiny side-room, where they would only be disturbed when their food was delivered.

"Did you see the wink he gave us? I think he got the wrong end of the stick." Tasha giggled.

Yvonne rolled her eyes but giggled back. "You're always getting me into trouble."

They ordered pasta and garlic bread and got down to business.

"You've already had the gist of these profiles from me. Most of this won't be new. All I've done is firmed them up ready for the team."

"Okay. So fire away."

"Rapist, first. He's going to be a reasonably intelligent male aged between twenty-five and fifty-five. Almost certainly a white-collar worker, given his taste in soap. He's a sexual predator who will have shown unusual tendencies from a young age. He'll have had a paraphilia of some description. There may have been a history of petty offending, possibly shoplifting or similar. There may have been an exposure offence."

"Which would put Ryan Smith in the frame, except he wasn't picked out by any of the victims this morning."

"This guy will perhaps still live with his mother but, if he's had relationships, none will have lasted for that long."

"What about the rapist-murderer?"

"Older - thirty-five to fifty-five. A high-functioning, intelligent individual with a considerable amount of personal charm. He's able to persuade savvy businessmen to take potentially unreasonable risks. He may be in a steady relationship or married but his partner isn't enough, and he'll have been rough with her, and there will be, almost certainly, a level of domestic abuse possibly spilling into violence."

The waiter laid their meals on the table, and poured half a bottle of water into their respective glasses.

Tasha continued. "He's most likely a businessman and, if not the boss, then reasonably high up in his organisation. Able to take time out when he needs it. He uses that time to stalk his victims and befriend the businessmen. This guy may have been clever enough to have evaded the law in the past, but he *will* have started on a much smaller scale. So, he too will have started with paraphillias, and perhaps petty crime."

"Good work." Yvonne sipped her water. "When are you presenting these to the team?"

"Tomorrow, the DCI said I must concentrate on the rapist profile."

"No more than I expected." Yvonne grabbed a bit of her garlic bread.

"What's your next move?" Tasha began eating her carbonara.

"I'm requesting the client files from Williams and West. I'm hoping there's something in there that'll get this case moving again."

Tasha nodded. "Might be worth speaking to the accountants who were used by the dead men."

"Callum and Dewi looked into that. Nothing found of any interest there. The accountants lost, out too. Quite a chunk of their income disappeared with the deaths."

"Of course..."

"I believe the perp created those financial losses as a way to get intimate access to the victims and their families."? Yvonne mouthed a fork full of pasta.

"He wanted the wives but raped other females because he couldn't actually have them, until the ultimate act of control when he could invade their bedrooms and take their lives." Tasha looked to the window.

"Yes..." The DI put down her knife and fork, eating at that moment felt wrong.

"He probably envied everything the businessmen had. So, he may have tried and failed at big business himself. Or maybe he's employed by such a businessman and can't get the big break he would like - the promotion he was promised, or something of that nature."

Yvonne finished chewing a mouthful of seafood pasta. "Then there's the masonic connection. Both Ben Davies and Tony Ball were masons. I believe the dead men attended the Masonic Temple in Newtown but I need confirmation of that. That's all we know at the moment, but they'll have lists of members so we can check it out."

"Will they give you the names?"

"More than that, hopefully... Well, that's the plan. We'll start with speaking to the lodge secretary at the temple. I have no idea if anything will come of it, but any information that adds to our understanding of the victims is a bonus. What was really going on in the minds of both men? The wider we cast our net the better."

"Understand the victims, understand the killer," Tasha agreed.

BACK AT THE STATION, Yvonne found Dewi going through the statements of the rape victims. Looking for anything they might have missed. "Aha, ma'am. Where were you? I've been searching all over for you."

"Sorry, Dewi, I left with Tasha for lunch. We went at short notice. I should have told you."

"It's okay. I just wanted you to know that Paul Baker's been in touch."

"Paul Baker, as in Williams and Wells?"

"That's the one, he's bringing in the files they have for Davies, Ball and Bennett."

"Well, that's great."

"He sounded nervous on the phone. Something tells me he may not have Darryl Williams' permission."

"What time is he coming in?"

"Later this afternoon, ma'am, he wasn't sure exactly when he'd be able to get away."

"Good, we've got time to dash over to the Masonic Hall on Milford Road. I've asked the lodge secretary to meet us there."

"Right you are, ma'am."

The Georgian, iron gate was painted pale-blue, and was far more intricately detailed than any other gate she'd seen on Milford Road. Yvonne turned the knob and pushed it open. It gave way with a well-oiled smoothness.

The building itself was pretty ordinary, save for the 'square and compass' symbol adorning the top. Gold implements on a blue-circle background, timeless symbols of the masons.

Dewi followed close behind her, his hands pushed deep into his long, summer raincoat. The DI was glad of his presence. Masonic temples were not usually the haunt of women. She was nervous about the reception she'd get.

Huw Williams greeted them at the door. A small man, at five-foot-four, he wasn't how the DI had pictured him. In her head, the Masonic lodge secretary would be a six-foot tall, strapping man in flowing, masonic robes.

The unassuming man in spectacles, greeting them with a warm smile, was the antithesis of this vision. She estimated him to be around fifty years of age.

"DI Yvonne Giles," she said, taking the offered hand.

He was still holding her hand when he turned towards Dewi, only letting go when the DS thrust his hand towards him.

"Come on in. I'm Huw, secretary and general dogsbody." He smiled and winked at Yvonne, and motioning them through. "Tea? I have coffee if you prefer."

Yvonne had done a little research, and new that the lodge secretary was a very important position. It carried a great deal of responsibility. She was impressed with the humility shown by Huw.

"Coffee please, milk no sugar." She smiled warmly back.

"Now, how can I help you?" Huw asked, once they were seated.

"We're interested in two men who were members of your lodge: Ben Davies and Tony Ball." Yvonne searched Huw's face.

Huw sighed, and looked down into his coffee mug, furrows lining his forehead. "That was a bad business."

"We're seeking closure for the families and friends – trying to piece together the last six months of their lives. Discovering why they might have made the decision to take their entire families with them."

"They were both members of the Provincial Grand Lodge of North Wales. Ben had been a member for about five years. Tony, let's see, Tony for about three years."

"Did they come to this temple regularly?"

"They came to most meetings. I think they only missed when they were off on some big business meeting. Many of our members are similar. People get involved when they can."

"Did they come here together?"

"Not together, no, Ben Davies was a member of Hafren Lodge. Hafren has a around fifty members. Tony was a member of Cedewain Lodge. There's almost eighty members of Cedewain."

"I see..."

"They were good men, Inspector. They did a lot of great work for the round table in Newtown and sponsored events and stalls for the Newtown carnival. They also helped schools and hospitals with equipment from time-to-time. They didn't deserve what happened to them."

"Were you surprised at them taking their own lives?"

"Honestly? Very..."

"Could you have foreseen them hurting their families?"

"No. I was shocked. We all were. We sign up to the masons to do good work. We all believe in God, or at least in a power higher than ourselves. Our core values are truth, charity and love. We help each other. None of us saw this coming. If we had, we'd have done everything in our power to prevent it."

"Did they talk to you, or anyone else in the lodge, about their financial difficulties?"

"They didn't discuss them with me. They may have discussed them with others. We held a special ceremony for them after they passed. No-one mentioned anything. Like I said, we were shocked. I didn't hear of anyone who saw it coming."

"How were the men introduced to the lodge?"

"Another member put them forward, originally."

"Can you remember who?"

"I can for Tony. I'd have to check my records as regards Ben."

"Who introduced Tony?"

"A gentleman called Darryl Williams."

"Darryl Williams the financial adviser?"

"I believe he is a financial adviser, yes."

"Would you check your records, when you get time, and let me know who introduced Ben?"

"Of course. Is it relevant?"

"We'd like to talk to as many people as possible. People who knew the men and may have known of their situation. Get a more complete picture," Dewi spoke up for the first time, having been busy getting down the notes.

"Oh, I see." Huw nodded his understanding.

"I'd appreciate it if you kept our conversation private." Yvonne finished the last mouthful of her coffee.

"If you wish, Inspector?"

"Thank you, Huw. The North Wales Lodge has the reputation of being one of the most closed lodges. You have been very helpful today, and for that we are really grateful."

Huw smiled, sadly. "It's the least I could do, under the circumstances."

"So, Darryl Williams introduced both men to the lodge." Dewi opened the gate for Yvonne as they headed back to their car.

"He seems to be cropping up everywhere." Yvonne paused, in the middle of opening her car door. "I think we need to find out a good deal more about our Mr Williams."

. . .

PAUL BAKER STOOD UP, as soon as Yvonne entered reception. He appeared furtive, looking through the window to the car park, as though checking he hadn't been followed. The DI held out her arm, pointing him towards the inner sanctum. She led him through to interview room one.

"This isn't a formal interview and I'm not recording," the DI stated, as she pulled a chair out for Paul to take a seat. "You asked to see me."

Paul Baker loosened the tie which was perfectly coordinated with the grey, sharp-suit he was wearing. Yvonne noticed his square-toed, black shoes. They had a good shine.

"I've brought you the list of our clients," he said, shifting as though someone had left pins on his seat.

"Thank you." Yvonne took the photocopied list from him. "Is something wrong?" she asked. "Are you worrying about something?"

"I'm fine," he said, rather too quickly.

"Darryl doesn't now you've brought this, does he?" she asked, realising this might be why he appeared uncomfortable.

"No., we keep our client's information confidential. If our clients lose faith in our ability to do that, we could lose them."

"What else are you holding, there?"

"These are the files for Ben Davies, Tony Ball and Robert Bennett. I thought you might like to look through them. Photocopy anything you feel relevant to your enquiries."

"What would Darryl do if he discovered you'd brought this files here?"

"I don't know, but it probably wouldn't be good for me."

"So, why did you risk it?"

"The men are dead. They can't object to their information being read."

"But you still didn't inform Darryl..."

"I'll tell him if he asks me. He has a temper, you know."

"Have you crossed him before?"

"We've had our disagreements."

"Did he talk to you about our visit to your offices?"

"He did."

"What did you talk about?"

"He asked me what I'd told you. Asked me if I'd strayed off-piste."

"So, he'd had a conversation with you before we arrived that day? Setting out what you could and couldn't tell us, to guarantee you were on-message?"

"Will the client list be helpful?"

"Are there people on this list who are currently losing money?"

"I don't know. I could try to find out."

"It's okay, I don't want you to risk further trouble. We could try to find that information for ourselves."

"I'd better go."

"Can we hold onto the men's files for a day or two?"

"Yes. I doubt Darryl will miss them in the short-term. He'll probably clear them from the records room eventually."

"Thanks for doing this." Yvonne put a hand in his shoulder. "If you become worried about your safety, get in touch with us straight away."

"My safety?" Baker looked confused. Yvonne immediately regretted saying anything.

"I'm not saying you should, I'm saying if you do. Don't worry about it. It doesn't matter."

Paul headed for the door. "I'll pick the files up again

when you've finished with them." Then he was gone. She saw him again, hastily getting into his car. She watched the car drive away, her interest piqued.

She found Dewi getting ready to leave for home. "Paul Baker is scared of Darryl Williams. He won't say why, but he's definitely on edge."

"You don't expect a partner, even a junior partner, to be afraid of the senior to that extent. Want me to bring Williams in for formal questioning?"

"And question him about what? We haven't got enough, yet. We do now have the client list, though. You get off, Dewi. I'll speak to you tomorrow, about checking out the list."

"You off home too, ma'am? It's been a long day..."

"Soon, Dewi, Soon."

IT WAS PAST SIX-THIRTY PM. The rest of the team had long since left for home. Yvonne leaned against the edge of her desk, gazing out over the car park, in the direction of Dolerw – the town public park. Her furrowed forehead and pale knuckles, as she gripped the edge of the desk, betrayed the strain she was under.

DCI Llewellyn knocked on the door of the office, even though he was already in the room. He didn't want to make her jump.

"I have two steaming mugs of hot chocolate," he said with a grin, as she turned towards him. "Freshly made, not from the machine."

Ordinarily, she would have smiled back, but her tired mind had not quite switched over from her previous train-of-thought. She rubbed her eyes and looked up at him. He thought, in that moment, that she might cry. She didn't, however.

"Thank you," she whispered, taking the mug from him and setting it down next to her. "That's very thoughtful."

Llewellyn perched on the other side of her, such that he, too, was now gazing in the direction of Dolerw Park. "You know, it all works out in the end. Good or bad, everything eventually gets concluded."

"I'd like to think so," she responded, her voice soft.

"You know, you're a curious mixture. There are times when you come into my office, eyes blazing, full of conviction and fighting tooth-and-nail for what you believe to be right." He turned his head, to search her face. "And then there are times, such as now, when I can see that you are riddled with self-doubt. Times when I think I have never seen someone look quite so worried about everything."

Yvonne blew on the top of her chocolate. "I really thought that either Mark Grantham or Ryan Smith would be picked out of that line-out. Why did I get so hung up on them?" She took a sip and sighed. "This chocolate *is* very good."

"Something about them obviously made you feel they could be involved."

"I thought they were hiding something."

"They may very well be hiding something. I doubt people get to the powerful positions they occupy, without have a few skeletons in their closet - just perhaps not literally."

"I think they may have taken advantage of the predicament that Ben Davies and the others found themselves in. I just no longer believe that they set them up."

"Do you need to take some time out? A week or two of annual leave, perhaps."

"No." She said it without hesitation, her voice firm. "I may not be sure, right now, what is going on, but I sure as hell know that something is, and I have to get to the bottom of it. If I have any doubts, its about my ability to get to the bottom of it fast enough to save the next victims."

Llewellyn nodded. "I can tell you that I don't share your doubt. If a killer is at work here, I have every faith that you'll stop him."

"I don't want to cause trouble for you from those higher up." She stood, and took her mug to the window.

"I think you should go home and rest. The case will still be here tomorrow." He finished his drink and turned for the door. "That's where I'm going now. Home."

"Thank you for the chocolate," Yvonne turned around to face him, "and for your support."

He smiled at her. "You're a very intelligent and beautiful woman. I'm lucky to have you on my team. You'll do this. Now...go home."

TASHA HAD GONE TO BED. Yvonne strolled into the Kitchen and pulled open the fridge. Inside, she found a glass of sauvignon blanc and a bowl of pasta, attached to which was a note telling her to warm the food up in the microwave. She smiled at her friend's thoughtfulness and carried the bowl and glass to the photo-wall, Tasha had named 'the maverick wall'.

In front of her were the photographs, flow charts, names and dates important to the case. Her mind was still working overtime, trying to piece it all together. What was she missing?

As other lines of enquiry faded, one name stood out for her. The arrows leading to it increased almost daily. Darryl

Williams. She felt sure that Paul Baker was scared of him. He'd introduced at least two of the dead men to the masons. He'd socialised with all of the dead men and, almost surely, had suggested to them that they invest in the deals which ultimately cost them everything.

She could kick herself for not having included him in the line-up. The disappointment of the last one meant she'd have to wait a while before organising another. She couldn't put the women through that experience again, not without being sure it was him. There was nothing in his past: no conviction or caution – either sexual or non-sexual. He was clean as a whistle.

The DI switched on the TV, for the local news, and settled on the sofa with her food and wine. She didn't expect anything on the family deaths. Murder-suicides didn't occupy the headlines long, unlike serial murders. There was nothing on the rapes, either. All quiet. The world was happily carrying on, oblivious to the rapist-killer waiting to take his next victims.

She breathed deeply, allowing the wine to relax her. She managed half the food. It was very good, but her appetite hadn't been the best of late. Death had that effect. Just before sleep took over, she climbed the stairs to bed.

PAUL BAKER'S mobile phone rang and rang.

"Can you talk?" Yvonne asked him, when he finally picked up.

"Hang on."

She heard a huff and scrape and some muffled voices. More huffing and scraping and then he was back.

"Okay, sorry about that. We can talk now."

"I'm sorry to bother you, but I'd like to know if any of

your current clients is in financial difficulty. Would you be able to come and see us, and indicate on the list you gave me, anyone who is losing money?"

There was a couple of seconds silence on the other end.

"Mr. Baker?"

"Yes, alright, I should ask Darryl's permission."

"I'd rather you didn't do that."

" I see. Do you suspect him of being a factor in Ben Davies' and Tony Ball's suicides?"

"I don't know. We're still trying to work it all out. I'd appreciate you keeping it to yourself, for now."

21

Tasha was deep in conversation with the DCI. Yvonne could see them through his office window. Whatever they were discussing, their meeting appeared amicable. The last time she'd seen them like that in his office, he was taking the psychologist off a case. That time, she'd stormed out. This time, he evidently wasn't sending her away. Good.

"Penny for them, ma'am." Dewi put a mug of tea on the desk for her.

"Darryl Williams."

"Err, no. Dewi Hughes."

"Ha ha." Yvonne smiled, in spite of herself. "What do you make of him?"

"He's risen to the top of your suspect list, hasn't he?"

"Paul Baker is jumpy about something. He's fairly loyal to his senior partner, though."

"Guess he values his job..."

"There's something Baker's not telling us. I've asked him to come in again, today. I'm asking him to indicate, on their client list, anyone losing money."

"Think he'll do it? We don't have a warrant. We couldn't use the list in evidence."

"I don't want the list for evidence, Dewi. I want to know who we should be concerned about."

"Confidential information..."

"Versus families' lives and young women not being raped."

"Point taken."

"I want you and Tasha to observe the discussion I have with him."

"Give me a shout when he gets here."

"Will do."

Tasha surfaced from Llewellyn's office and headed straight to Yvonne.

"Everything okay?" the DI asked, still sipping on the tea Dewi had given her.

"Everything's fine, thank you. The DCI was asking about the profile I prepared for you. Wanted my take on the whole murder-suicide versus family killer thing."

"What did you say?"

"That I am in agreement with you, about pretty much everything."

"What does he think?"

"Tells me he has every faith in our judgement. Wants me to keep my eye on you."

"Really?"

"I think he thinks you might do something risky."

"Does he, indeed?"

"I think he likes you."

"Haven't you got something to do?"

Tasha laughed. "Yes, I've got to give a briefing to the team."

"Good." Yvonne smiled, then: "I like being single."

Tasha turned to leave.

"Oh, I almost forgot." Yvonne put a hand on her arm. "I'll be talking with Paul Baker from Williams and West, later. I'd like you and Dewi to observe."

"You got it." Tasha nodded and left to prepare for the team briefing.

Paul Baker's tie was loosely knotted, the top button of his shirt was undone, and his hair was not quite as slick as it usually was. He checked behind him, as he entered the station.

Yvonne greeted him in reception and took him through to the interview room, taking in the change in his appearance.

"Thank you for coming in again. I know you're a busy man. I've brought the client list with me, for you to look at."

"Can I ask you why you want the names from me? It's dodgy ground, I'm treading – data protection and all that."

"I didn't get a warrant for the information. I'm just interested in protecting those who might be at risk of taking their own lives..."

"Are you going to compile client lists from *every* financial advice firm?"

"Just the ones in my jurisdiction."

"I see." He appeared doubtful, his eyes narrow.

"Look," Yvonne sighed, "those men didn't just kill themselves. They took their wives and their children with them."

"I know..." He looked down at his shoes, shifting his weight between his feet.

"Most of the children were tiny...toddlers."

He continued gazing downwards.

"I couldn't protect them, but I can be prepared to protect families in the future. Make sure that counsellors are on hand."

"We suggest counsellors to our clients. They don't always take us up on that."

"In that case, we can take the next steps."

"Next steps?" He looked up at her now, hands in his jacket pockets.

"Revoke any gun licences they may hold. This is a rural area. Many of the farming and land-owning families have gun cabinets. That's an issue, if there are family members who are feeling suicidal."

He swept his hands down his face. "Okay, what do you need to know."

"I'd like you to look down the client list you gave me and underline those who are suffering serious financial losses."

He nodded and started scouring the list. When he'd finished, three clients had been underlined. Their addresses were in Machynlleth, near the coast; Dolfor, five miles from Newtown; and Hendomen, near to Montgomery.

Yvonne took the list from him. "Thank you, Mr. Baker."

"You won't tell these families that I gave you the information?"

"We have ways of keeping our sources anonymous." The DI gave him a reassuring smile.

"Thank you. Can I go now?"

"Yes, of course." Yvonne showed him out of the building.

"So, WHAT DO YOU THINK?" she asked Dewi and Tasha, when they re-grouped. "Nervous, wasn't he?"

"Well, he was giving you confidential information without the say-so of his senior. I think that was bound to put him on edge. Hell, I'd be on edge if I was giving out info without speaking to you." Dewi ran his hand through his hair.

"Tasha?" Yvonne looked at the psychologist.

"I think he's hiding something. Did you see the way he avoided eye contact when you spoke about depression and the possibility of revoking gun licences?"

"I'm inclined to agree with both of you and, yes, I did notice his looking down."

"Does he have a gun licence?" Tasha crossed her arms. "Is he suffering with depression?"

"I certainly don't think everything is rosy at Williams and Wells," Yvonne answered with a sigh. "I just don't know why, yet."

"I can make discreet enquiries." Dewi wrote a few notes in his pad.

"He's given us the names and addresses of three men, living in the area, who are losing substantial sums of money." Yvonne directed the next at Dewi: "I want discreet protection assigned to all three addresses. It'll have to be uniform, in the main, but I want CID around, too. I want to know who is coming and going and, if there's anything suspicious about any of the visitors, particularly late evening or night-time visitors, I want the alarm raised."

"Right you are, ma'am."

"Okay, let's get the team together. Tasha's going to give her profile to everyone. I want copies of it to go to protection officers assigned to those addresses."

Yvonne had shaken off some of the cobwebs and doubts that had been nagging at her. She felt things were finally moving.

22

He pulled on a dark, hooded raincoat, over a light t-shirt. The weather had dodged between rain and sunshine all day. He was prepared for both.

The bulging clouds threatened a storm but had not yet released their anger. Ripples of electricity ran through the hairs on his skin, like the scraping of sharp nails. Storms excited him.

He'd driven for nearly an hour. The air-con in his car needed fixing, and the humidity had been claustrophobic. He took his rucksack from the boot and headed off along the path. The boots he wore could be bought from most stores, a dime-a-dozen. Not his usual choice, but they'd render any footprints meaningless.

A light drizzle misted the way and began smudging out the horizon to his right. He walked quickly, impatient to see the house, again. Impatient to see *her*.

He heard the engine just before the vehicle swung around the corner, its headlights slicing through the drizzle-mist. He threw himself behind vegetation, just in time, his heart bursting in his chest. He recognised the car. The husband had left the house.

He breathed deeply to calm himself. That had been close. Careless. He lifted himself up and brushed off the damp grass, weeds and most of the mud. He righted the rucksack on his back and continued walking to his favourite viewing spot.

The lights of the house glowed orange and pale blue, through the darkening mist. He crouched low, taking the bag off his back and pulling from it his binoculars, and a HD digital recorder. It would now be a question of endurance. Him, versus the drizzle.

She was putting the kids to bed, reading them a bedtime story. He caught fleeting glimpses of her, as she tucked them up. She dimmed the lights in their rooms and drew the curtains. He'd wait for her to reappear in one of the downstairs rooms, most likely the kitchen-diner.

He closed his eyes for a moment, imagining what he might do to her, given the chance. Violent, filthy things, involving the kitchen island and the floor. Things he would never actually get to do. This could only play-out one way.

He was disappointed that she wasn't in her underwear, like last time. She was wearing a light, cotton dress, her hair still in a ponytail after a busy day with the children. School holidays. She stood, rubbing her back and stretching. He had to breathe deep again.

He shifted his weight, as one elbow was losing all feeling. He stretched the arm, the bones clicking from the damp, and replaced the binoculars to his face. She'd disappeared again.

What he wasn't expecting, was what happened next. Another set of headlights approaching through the mist.

This time, from the opposite direction. The light came on in the shower-room.

The intruder-car pulled into the driveway, the automatic security lights beaming down. It wasn't the husband, and he'd brought wine. The watcher didn't know who this man was. He only knew that he hated him.

SARAH FINISHED HER SHOWER, unaware of the watcher outside in the developing darkness. It had been a long day. Three children, under the age of eight, home for the holidays. As much as she adored them, everything ached, from her feet to her neck.

A hot power-shower and pine-scented gel helped relax her. She put on a white, silk robe and padded barefoot to the door.

Her brother stood there pretending to be asleep. She giggled and slapped him lightly on the arm. He gave her a bear-hug, lifting her bodily off the floor and carrying her inside.

She smiled the widest she had all evening, and watched as he opened one of her sleek, kitchen drawers and took out a bottle-opener.

"What sort of a day have you had?" he asked, taking two large glasses from an overhead cupboard.

"Tiring, you?" She leaned back against the counter-top.

"Busy. I didn't feel like going back to the flat just yet." He poured liberally from the bottle of merlot.

"You and Christine still not back together, then?"

"She says she won't have me back, this time." He sighed, joining his sister in leaning against the counter-top. "She will, though. She can't resist me." He grinned from ear-to-ear.

"You need to prioritise her a little more – less going out drinking with your mates."

"Yeah, yeah, you said." He winked at his sister, who would have given him another friendly slap, except that her three-year-old boy had appeared in the kitchen doorway, rubbing his eyes and dragging his teddy. He called for her in a voice that betrayed how close he was to crying. She scooped him up onto her hip, and returned to leaning against the kitchen units. The little one snuggled into her neck, rapidly falling back to sleep.

"You eaten?" she asked her brother.

He shook his head.

"What would you like?"

"One of your amazing mixed-pepper and ham omelettes."

"You cuddle this little bundle back to bed, and I'll rustle you one up."

OUTSIDE, the watcher had seen enough. He seethed with a mixture of excitement and rage. He envied this man, whoever he was. He rammed his binoculars back into the rucksack, slung it over his back, and headed into the mist.

DEWI FOUND Yvonne getting herself a drink from the water-dispenser, a faraway look in her eyes.

"Ma'am, I've found the name of a female ex-employee of Williams and West. Someone who left the company under a cloud."?

"Really? Who? When? Why?"

"Seven years ago, she'd alleged sexual harassment against..."

"Darryl Williams?" Yvonne straightened up, eyes gleaming.

"You guessed it."

"And he wasn't prosecuted for it?"

"No. It went to a tribunal, but the panel decided there was no case to answer. They did, however, issue a warning to Williams as regards future conduct. Conduct that could be misread."?

"We should find her and talk to her."

"I'll look into it, ma'am."

23

His insides writhed, with an explosive mix of excitement and rage. He left the bed-and-breakfast, on the corner of the harbour, having hardly touched his food.

He paused, looking across the water, in the direction of the house. He couldn't see it from where he was. A hill and monument obscured the view.

He turned on his heel, having already decided to walk to the university campus: less risk of his car being picked up on CCTV. At his pace, it took a mere twenty minutes for him to access the campus. He went the back route, via the hospital car park. He took the path that wended around the outside, finally getting to the back of the Arts Centre. He took a side alley into the square, and into the front of the centre.

"Darjeeling."

The waitress looked up sharply. There was an arrogance to the order, but his face was passive.

"Coming right up," she answered casually. She took her time making the tea. "If you want milk, it's over there." She tossed the words over her shoulder.

"Sugar?" He barked the question. He didn't want sugar, but how dare she turn her back on him.

"Next to the milk." Again, she said the words without looking at him, sealing her fate.

He hung around, out of sight, until she finished her shift. Then followed her as she made her way back to her hall of residence. Now he knew where she lived, he walked back down Penglais Hill. He'd be back. Later.

"MA'AM, CAN I HAVE A WORD?" Callum asked, as he ran down the corridor.

"Can it wait, Callum? I was just on my way to see the DCI."

"I think you'll want to hear this: Aber have just been in touch. There's been another rape, just off the university campus. The girl was dragged into college-owned woods, just across road from her halls of residence. MO fits with our offender."

"Did he smell of soap?"

"Err..." Callum checked his notes. "He didn't smell of sweat or strong odours. Just smelled clean, apparently."

"I see."

"The description of what he was wearing would fit with our previous rapes."

"Who was the victim?"

"A law student who works part-time at the cafe in the arts centre, apparently."

"Get a car, Callum. Also, could you find Dewi and Tasha and ask them to come with us? We'll speak to Aber CID and take a look at the crime scene."

"Will do, ma'am."

. . .

"We're dealing with a very mobile perp," Tasha mused aloud, gazing out over the countryside, as the car sped along Cemmaes Road.

"How can he afford all this time for stalking?" Dewi shook his head.

"There's a family in danger." Yvonne rubbed her face. "When we get back, I want to go through the client list Paul Baker gave us. I want to remind myself of who is losing money, in the Aberystwyth area. We'll need to put double the protection on their homes."

"Will the DCI agree that?" Dewi looked doubtful.

"He'll need the go-ahead from higher up. It'll require using more uniformed officers from Aber." Yvonne pulled a face. "We were ready to put protection on the homes of all Williams and West clients who are losing money. That's what I wanted to talk to the DCI about. That would have taken *more* persuasion. This way we're potentially narrowing down to one house."

They entered the campus via the turn-off from Penglais Hill, stopping at the security barrier. Yvonne de-camped and spoke to the guard, showing her ID. He told her where they could park and confirmed with her that Aber officers had already taken the CCTV footage from the cameras.

They exited the main campus on foot, the way they'd come in. Dodging the heavy traffic on the main road, they crossed to the other side and the gateway to Penglais Woods, via Botany Gardens. Lines of police tape still hung here and there, from the ongoing investigation. They followed the common-approach path which had been marked out for investigators.

"So, the girl was on her usual jog route." Yvonne looked around her, and took a couple of pictures with her mobile.

"That's right." Callum caught her up. "She works in the

arts centre cafe, on the days when she's not studying. She does the run most nights, around dusk - prior to it being fully dark."

"She's a brave girl." As they reached the downward pathway through the wood, the DI began to picture it with the light fading. She shivered.

"It's no more than a few minutes worth of jogging, from here." Dewi pointed in the direction they were headed. "She'd be in Aber town centre and then the sea front, in no more than ten or fifteen minutes.

"So, he was waiting for her and knew her routine." Tasha rubbed the back of her neck.

"He must have watched her, prior to the attack." Yvonne nodded. "But if jogging was part of her evening routine, he wouldn't have needed to watch her for long."

The woodland path was around six feet wide, with trees at regular intervals. Sparsely lit, it was an ideal place for the attack, when compared to any other part of the student's route.

"You think he's watching a family in the area, too?" Tasha turned to face the DI.

"I know he is. I believe the family is most likely to be one known to Williams and West. The father will have been making heavy losses on his investments."

"How long is the interval between the rapes and the family deaths?" Tasha peered at the taped-off square of ground, where the attack took place.

"Not long, we're talking weeks. Maybe only a couple of weeks. I'll talk to the DCI today about night-time protection." Yvonne crouched close to the flattened grass. "She'd have been terrified."

"She put up a fight, apparently. None of her punches connected properly, unfortunately," Callum said, joining them. "His punch knocked the victim out long enough for him to bring her under his control."

The DI shivered again and turned to continue down the hill, Tasha walking alongside her.

"Tasha, why would he be raping these girls and yet murdering the families? Is it because he cannot have the married women?"

"This is a complex perp. He feels murderous rage and lust and has the urge to both rape and kill. He would combine the acts, if he thought he could get away with it. By separating them, he makes it less likely he'll be caught. He's protecting himself. This perp has a lot to lose. His fear of the loss of his reputation is the only thing that would have stopped him killing this girl."

"Do you think he just picks someone at random to rape, when he's watching families?"

"Well, it's possible the girls anger him in some way. Callum said the victim works part-time in the arts centre. He may have seen her there. Perhaps she didn't serve him in the way he wanted, or maybe he likes choosing his victims in cafes and pubs. Remember the Montgomery victim?"

"Tina Pugh. Yes, working in a cafe in the town."

"He watches the families, maybe staying in a hotel or sleeping in his car, he goes to cafes for his meals. He's feeling worked up, having spied on the females in their homes. Perhaps he takes out his sexual frustration on the girls who serve him his meals." Tasha shrugged. "It's a theory."

"Brilliant, Tasha. It makes sense. We have to get a move on. We have very little time until he claims his next family."

Yvonne poured over the list, given to her by Paul Baker.

"Who are we looking at?" Dewi asked, plopping some papers on the desk.

"I think we can rule out Dolfor and Hendomen. That just leaves Machynlleth and a client named Neil Thomas."

"How far is Machynlleth from Aberystwyth?"

"Well, looking on Google, about seventeen miles. It's the Aber side of Mach, and so I'm estimating about fifteen miles. Fifteen miles from the attack in Aber to the Thomas household."

"It's got to be that one." Dewi's forehead furrowed. "We'd better get people on it."

"Here's what I want you to do, Dewi. Task one of the team to do overnight surveillance. I'd say seven pm until seven am should cover it. They'll need to take at least one uniform PC with them. I'll get permission from the DCI for the operation."

"I'm on it, ma'am."

"Set it up now. I don't think Llewellyn will refuse. Then we'll get back together and go and see Karen Jones, the ex-employee of Williams and West. Let's find out what it was that Darryl Williams was alleged to have done."

SHE CAUGHT Chris Llewellyn leaving his office.

"Sir, can I have a word?"

"Yvonne, can it wait I've..."

"I'm sorry, it's urgent."

He could see the earnest look in her eyes. "Very well, how can I help?"

"I need to put overnight protection on a house just outside of Machynlleth. It will need to be discreet. I don't think it would be right to worry the family: in case we've got it wrong."

"You'd better give me some detail, and quick." The DCI put his hands on his hips.

Yvonne filled him in about the Aber rape and her theory.

"Does Tasha agree with you on this?"

The DI raised an eyebrow. "Yes."

"Okay. I'll agree it, but it'll have to also be agreed with Aber CID. They may help out with personnel."

"Thank you, sir." Yvonne gave a sigh of relief.

"How long do you think you'll need the protection detail for?"

"Weeks, rather than months, sir."

"Right."

"There's something else. I hope to interview an ex-employee of my main suspect today or tomorrow, at the latest. Alleged sexual harassment which was never prosecuted."

"I see."

"If it confirms my suspicions, I'll be asking your permission to put a tail on him."

"Consider that permission granted." The DCI smiled at her. "Go get him."

Yvonne smiled back, before turning on her heel and running down the corridor.

She found Dewi, about to make a phone call.

"Get a tail on Darryl Williams, too." She winked at her DS.

"Really? I'm on it." Dewi put his thumbs up.

24

Karen Jones was now a hospital administrator, working for Shrewsbury and Telford Trust. Yvonne and Dewi caught up with her in Shrewsbury Hospital. She'd asked a colleague to cover for her whilst she spoke with the detectives.

They were granted a side-room off of one of the wards, and sat down in the chairs usually earmarked for patients and visitors. The bed next to them was empty.

"Karen, thank you for agreeing to speak to us." The DI took out her note pad. "We'd like to talk to you about your time working for Williams and West. I understand you alleged sexual harassment against the CEO, Darryl Williams."

"Alleged? He did harass me." Her cheeks flushed. "I've filled out a bit since then," she said, referring to her ample size. "Just because he got off with it, doesn't mean he didn't do it. That man has friends in high places." She screwed her face up, an obvious indication of her disgust.

"How long had you worked for the company?"

"I was in my late teens when I started there. Let's see

now..." She tilted her head to one side, looking downwards for a moment, then: "About six-and-a-half years."

"And when, would you say, the harassment began?"

"Oh, right off the bat."

"As soon as you began working there?" Yvonne wrote busily in her book.

"Definitely, within the first six months." Karen peered at the DI's pad, as though checking everything was being noted correctly. "He's harassed someone else, hasn't he? I knew it. I knew he'd do it again. I told them that."

"Told who?"

"The tribunal."

"Mrs Jones, he hasn't been accused of anything. We are investigating a separate matter, and he is just one of the people we are interested in. We are looking into all of their backgrounds. We are not at liberty to tell you what we are investigating."

"But he's done something..." Karen's eyes shone with triumph.

Yvonne put her pen to her lips, unsure of what to make of her.

"What did Mr Williams do to you, Mrs Jones?" Dewi asked his first question of the witness.

"He kept telling me his wife didn't understand him. Arranged for me to go with him to conferences, to get time alone with me."

"I understand you were his PA. Did that not mean you were *supposed* to go to conferences?" Yvonne's eyes narrowed.

"Some of them, yes, but not all the ones he asked me to."

"Anything else, Mrs Jones?"

"He'd come up behind me while I was typing. Hand me papers over my shoulder, to brush against my chest."

"Did you tell him you were uncomfortable with his invasion of your personal space?"

"No."

"How did you let him know you didn't like it?"

"I'd move away. Move back, like."

"Did he say anything to you?"

"He'd tell me that he liked my dress, or my shoes."

"I see..." Yvonne nodded.

"He kissed me at one of those conferences and ran his hands over my bottom and my chest." Karen said, rapidly. "He tried to force me into his room."

The DI stiffened. "Uninvited?"

"Completely out of the blue. We'd just returned from a conference dinner."

"Had he been drinking?"

"We'd both had a couple of glasses of wine, but nothing more than that."

"What did you do?"

"I hit him. Hard on both shoulders. I think I slapped his face."

"What did he do then?"

"He told me I wanted it. That he could tell I'd been coming onto him for weeks. I told him I just wanted to go to bed. Alone."

"What happened then?"

"He calmed down, asked if I would make him a coffee."

"And did you?"

"I did. With hindsight, I realised I shouldn't have. I just thought he'd had a moment of madness, fuelled by the wine."

"So you took him into your room." The question was not delivered in a judgemental way.

"I did."

"What happened next?"

"We began drinking coffee, sitting on the bed."

"On the bed?"

"There was nowhere else to sit." Karen shrugged. "Like I said, I thought his moment of madness was over."

"Are you telling us it wasn't?"

"Within a few minutes, he'd started again – wandering hands, trying to kiss me."

"Did he use force?"

"He pushed me down onto the bed and held my wrists above my head."

"And then?"

"I pushed him back and screamed. We were in a hotel. There were guests next door. He got up. He was breathing heavily. He left. He just left at that point."

"So, you filed a complaint the next day?"

"Well, it was a couple of months later that I actually made the complaint."

"Why the delay, Mrs Jones?"

"I kept mulling it over. Wondering if I'd led him on in any way."

"Why did the tribunal not find in your favour?"

"Like I said earlier, he's got friends in high places. Rich friends. All in cahoots with that masons business."

"Are you saying that you think the masons helped to get him off?"

"I know they did."

"Did you know any? Were there any you suspected of helping him at the time?"

"There were a few. Including one that was later charged with insider trading. They had a lot of hushed meetings around that revelation."

"Mrs Jones, if we need to, may we speak to you again?"

"Of course, Inspector. I'm more than happy to help the police."

"Thank you. You've been very helpful."

As they left the hospital, Yvonne turned to her DS. "Dewi, what did you make of her?"

"Seemed genuine enough, ma'am. She felt she was never going to get justice, so she didn't push for a prosecution."

"And we now have Darryl Williams attempting to use force on a young woman, his employee. Not only that, but this demonstrates him pre-planning the attack by taking her away to a conference."

"Could have been the start of a sex-offending career."

"Absolutely, she was a good find, Dewi, good job."

"Thank you, ma'am."

"Did you get the protection organised for the Machynlleth family?"

"I did ma'am. Aber colleagues are covering it, and Callum will be checking in with them on a regular basis."

"Okay, good. Let me know the minute there are any developments."

"Will do."

Callum was waiting for them when they got back. "Ma'am, we have CCTV footage that we believe is from the campus attacker."

"Thank goodness. Can I take a look?"

"I'm setting it up now, ma'am. Don't get too excited though," the DC warned, "Aber have already told us it's very grainy and the perp was wearing a hat."

He wasn't wrong. Excitement turned to disappointment

when they saw the state of the footage. The unsub was in the right place at the right time to be their perp but, try as they might, they just couldn't get a decent image of the face.

"Alright, get the footage to forensics and see what they can do with it. We should at least be able to get an approximate height and build of the suspect." Yvonne was already leaving her seat. "Tell them it's urgent."

"How is it going? Going to fill me in?" Tasha had a mug of coffee in each hand and was therefore forced to have the pack of biscuits gripped between her teeth,

Yvonne laughed at the garbled questions, taking the pack of biscuits from the psychologist's mouth. "I think I know what you just said to me."

"Sorry, need more hands." Tasha smiled.

The DI filled her in as regards the protection assignment, the tail on Darryl Williams, and the interview with Karen Jones.

"So, you've firmed up on Darryl as your main suspect?"

"Certainly have. Will you come in on the interview when we pull him in?"

"I wouldn't miss it."

Tonight was the night. Everything, from his watch to his shoes, had to be just so. He checked his Rolex again: Seven-thirty. He chose a pale-blue, rich-cotton shirt and a pair of semi-casual but expensive chinos. A dark-blue blazer finished the look.

After his shower, he had sparsely dotted his sandalwood cologne. He breathed deeply, taking a couple of seconds before letting the air slowly back out. He could feel his heart-rate slow, could feel the sweat on the small of his back.

"Want a digestive?"

"No, thanks. I'm all digestive'd out." DC Callum Jones had been sitting in the unmarked car for several hours with the Aberystwyth PC, Pete Long. It followed on from several lots of all-night vigils. In that time, he had gotten to know the man well : what he had for breakfast, his hobbies, the problems he'd been having with his car, and his plans for the weekend.

On top of this, the DC had eaten his way through the best part of a packet of custard creams and two bars of chocolate. The latter, he wasn't at all happy about. Now, the two men sat in bored silence.

Darryl Williams had gotten home early: four-thirty in the afternoon. That had meant they had started their vigil much earlier than usual. Uniform had given them the heads up just before five. It was now seven-thirty. It had been drizzling with rain for an hour, though it was still very warm. Every now and then Pete would flick the windscreen wipers, to clear their view of the house. Once or twice this made the dozing Callum, jump.

Pete had turned on the radio a couple of times, quickly turning it off when he saw the frown on the DC's face. Callum found it too much of a distraction.

"What d'you think he's doing in there?" Pete leaned right back in his seat, his legs splayed. With one hand, he was undoing the top button on his collar, to stop his neck chafing.

"Well, knowing our luck, probably watching TV or drinking bourbon." Callum sighed. He felt sticky and dirty after nearly four hours cooped up in the car.

"What would you be doing tonight, if we weren't here?"

"Seeing the girlfriend... She's not happy at the moment. Says she gets to see less and less of me."

"That true?"

"Yeah, yeah, it is. Our DI's got a bee in her bonnet over this one."

"Think she's barking up the wrong tree?"

"Dunno, yeah, Maybe." Callum regretted saying it, the moment the words left his mouth. Too late, he'd said it now. He eyed the PC, wondering of his doubts would be all around the Aberystwyth station, this time tomorrow.

He packed the essential items into his fold-over satchel: brand new atomiser, overshoes, two pairs of gloves and rags. He took a final look in the mirror. He was ready.

The meeting was set for eight o'clock, earlier than he would have liked. Still, he could make sure it lasted long enough for the rest of the family to give up and go to bed.

He placed a half-bottle of Laphroaig single malt into his bag, just in case. He breathed deeply again and left the house.

"Bloody hell, there he is." PC Pete sat up straight, pushing the dozing DC on the arm. "Wake up, mate. He's left the house."

Callum bolted upright, focusing his eyes through the windscreen drizzle and on the back of Darryl Williams, who was getting into his silver Lexus.

"Get ready," Callum ordered. "Follow him as soon as he sets off. I'll phone the DI."

. . .

Yvonne fumbled for her mobile. "DI Giles..."

"Ma'am, he's on the move."

"How's he dressed?"

"Like he's going off somewhere important."

"Good work, Callum. I'll get things sorted this end. Don't let him out of your sight."

She raced down the corridor and banged on DCI Llewellyn's door.

He opened it, just as she pushed. He stopped her from falling. "Good God, has somebody died?"

"Sir, can I have an ARV and dog unit on standby. Callum is on the tail of my main suspect, who looks to be on his way to a late night meeting."

"Are you heading after them?"

"That's the plan, yes."

"I'll get the teams on standby. As soon as you know where the suspect is headed, you let me know. And Yvonne?"

"Sir?"

"Don't do anything rash."

"No, sir."

"Keep me informed."

"Of course, sir."

"Every development."

"Sir."

"Dewi, can you find Tasha and ask her to meet us at the car in five." Yvonne checked the contents of her bag. "Make sure we have some spare mobiles."

"Will do." Dewi disappeared in search of the psychologist.

The DI's pounding blood whistled in her ears, as she put

a hand out onto the bonnet to steady herself. Another family could be at risk tonight. She'd lay money on the fact that Darryl Willams was on his way to Machynlleth. She saw it as her mission to save the family and put this rapist-killer behind bars. She thought of her nephew and niece and this galvanised her, staving off a threatening panic attack. She took a few long breaths and willed her body to stay calm.

TASHA WAS STILL TRYING to get her coat on as she got into the car. Yvonne had to help her out, holding one of the sleeves, whilst Tasha wriggled into it. The psychologist's eyes were shining and her cheeks were as red as her top. The DI felt a pang of self-doubt. What if she had this wrong?

As though sensing Yvonne's reticence, Tasha put a hand on her elbow. "Come on, we've been working hard for this."

Yvonne nodded and got in the passenger seat. Dewi drove.

TEN MINUTES LATER, and Callum called over the radio. "He's approaching Mach. Approaching Mach, over."

"Is he heading for the Williams house, over?"

"He's taking a left, left, left into...yes. He's on the lane leading to the Williams house."

"Keep on him. Don't let him disappear. Eyes on him throughout."

"Understood, over."

The DI chewed her thumb, her gut tight; the sound of blood in her ears.

. . .

MILES DISAPPEARED without his noticing them. He mentally practised his moves and the things he would say. He played the anticipated master-bedroom scene over and over, his trousers tightening. He checked his Rolex. Seven forty-five.

He sped up a little. In his malaise, he'd let his speed slip and was in danger of arriving late. In the event, he arrived at the house five minutes early. *She* opened the door. He put his satchel in front of his loins. He could smell her scent as she led him to where her husband was waiting. It was with regret, that he watched her slip away to the kitchen.

25

Darryl Williams straightened his tie. "Michael." He smiled broadly, extending his arm, for the special handshake. He was shown to Michael's study and offered a seat in the Chesterfield. He sat down, but perched forward in the chair. He didn't want to get too comfortable.

"Before we get down to business..." Michael Williams wandered out of the room, returning with a pump-action shotgun. "What do you think of this beauty?"

Darryl accepted the gun from Michael's outstretched hands. "Wow, nice. Are you coming to the next shoot?"

"You betchya."

Darryl raised the gun, feeling the weight of it. Feeling the butt against his shoulder and putting an eye to the sight.

The noise of the door being hammered out of its jam, reverberated through the house like an explosion. Before he knew what was happening, Darryl's hands were pinned behind his back and he was eating carpet.

"Darryl Williams, I am arresting you on suspicion of attempted murder. You do not have to say-" Callum was out of breath, one knee in the back of the struggling Darryl Williams.

"Michael, Michael, what's going on?" An open-mouthed Mrs Williams was at the study door, a look of horror on her face.

"I don't know...officers?"

Callum, having finished giving the prisoner his rights, had begun hauling him off to the awaiting car. Pete Long talked to Michael and his wife for a few moments, reassuring them but giving little away. They saw him out, still confused.

"Ma'am, we got him. Gun-in-hand. We're on our way to Aberystwyth station, over."

"And the Wiliamses?"

"All okay, ma'am."

"Thank God, well done, Callum. I'll see you at the station. Don't interview him till we get there." Yvonne closed her eyes. "They've got him." Her forehead creased in a frown.

"What's the matter?" Tasha leaned between Dewi and the DI's seat.

"I just didn't expect it to be that easy." Yvonne shrugged. "Let's go talk to him."

THE KNOT of Darryl's tie was halfway down his chest, the top two buttons of his shirt undone. His sleeves were rolled up and his hair unkempt. Yvonne found him repeating to himself, over and over, "I don't believe it, I don't believe this is happening."

"Which bit don't you believe, Mr Williams?" The DI kept her tone firm and even.

"Has my solicitor arrived yet?" He looked up at her, he looked older.

"He's on his way."

"Why am I here?"

"I had hoped you might tell me the answer to that question."

"Attempted murder? What the hell is that about?"

"Mr Williams, I don't think you should say anymore until your solicitor arrives."

Yvonne knew they had to get this right and, besides, Tasha and Dewi had to be in place in the obs room. Plus, she wanted Callum, the arresting officer, in here as her co-pilot.

Her DC gave her a nod on his way in. "Solicitor's arrived in the station, ma'am."

Yvonne was relieved. The more time they gave Darryl Williams, the more opportunity he had to concoct a story. She cleared her throat as the attorney made his way to the table. "You've got fifteen minutes with him before we start."

"That's not much time." He puffed himself up.

"You can have more, later, if you need it," she said, leaving the room.

When she returned, she had Callum with her. She introduced everyone for the tape.

"My client would like to know why he has been arrested on suspicion of attempted murder."

Yvonne smiled. "He can add to that, suspicion of sexual assault."

"Sexual assault? What is this?" Darryl ran his hands through his hair, ending with them on top of his head, as though he could protect himself that way.

"I believe you were the employer of Karen Jones."

"Karen?"

"Yes, she alleges sexual assault against you. She states that you assaulted her over a period of several months and that you closed ranks with your masonic buddies to cover it up."

"Are you charging my client with that offence?"

"I want to put the questions to him."

"It's alright." Darryl sighed. "I'll answer her questions."

"Thank you, Mr Williams."

"Look, she harassed me. Stalked me, in fact."

"That's not how she sees it."

"Oh really? How *does* she see it? Which part of her sending me emails, asking me to leave my wife, was me harassing her?"

"Did you keep copies of the emails?"

"No, of course not. I was terrified my wife would find them."

"Why were you terrified, if you had nothing to hide?"

"My wife wasn't always rational."

"Karen alleges that you told her your wife doesn't understand you. Classic line, isn't it?"

"I didn't tell her that. Or, if I did, it wasn't in the context of trying to get her pants off."

"She said you persuaded her to go to conferences with you, to get time alone with her."

"She would offer to come, to help keep my notes in order and for me to practice my presentations on her."

"You tried to kiss her."

"I did not. She tried to kiss me. I swear."

"But you deleted the emails, your only evidence that Karen was stalking you."

"My marriage was on the rocks. I didn't want things made worse." Darryl sighed again, staring at the desk. "As it was, she left me anyway. The allegations against me were the last straw. I never found anyone else. I loved her. I still do. I'd have her back in a heartbeat."

Yvonne put several dates to him: the dates of the three rapes and when the families lost their lives.

"Where were you on those dates, Mr Williams?"

"Can I have a moment alone with my client?" The solicitor gave her a withering look.

"Okay, we'll take ten. But, when we reconvene, I'll want answers to those questions."

"What do you think, so far?" the DI asked Callum.

"His distress seems genuine. Either that, or he's a very good actor."

"Agreed, but he'd be distressed if he was guilty, wouldn't he?"

"Are you going to put the deaths of the families to him?"

"Let's see what he says about the dates. I'll put it to him that he was going to use that gun on the family and see what gives. Then I'd like to confer with Tasha and Dewi, in the obs room. To be honest, Callum, we haven't got much. They've searched his car and briefcase, and found nothing. If he doesn't confess, I don't know if we can get enough evidence for a conviction, except for the assaults against Karen Jones. That's why I put that to him. I thought we'd have more time to observe him in Michael Williams' house."

"I had to take him when I did, ma'am. He had the gun in his hands."

"I know, and I accept that. I just didn't expect him to have the gun so early in the evening. He changed the pattern. Did you get a statement from Michael Williams?"

"Not yet, ma'am."

"I'll speak to him after this interview. We need to know that circumstances under which the gun was handed over."

"Ma'am."

When the interview resumed, Darryl Williams was only able to tell them that he was at home on those dates. That he was probably working or watching telly.

Callum, after several nights of obs on the man, thought this might very well be true.

"Mr Williams, do you have any clients who are making heavy losses on the financial markets?"

"I have one client who has been incurring heavy losses."

"I put it to you that there are three of your clients making heavy losses, and one of them is Michael Williams."

"Michael Williams? What? Incurring losses? No way..."

"I put it to you that you orchestrated those losses."

"He's not in losing money."

"You orchestrated them with a view to taking advantage of his vulnerability."

"He's not incurring losses. Ask him."

Yvonne named the other two families on Paul Baker's list. "What about those men? They losing money too?"

"No." Darryl banged his hand on the table.

"Have you led them all into losing money."

"No."

"I object to you badgering my client." The solicitor stood up.

Yvonne held her hand up. "Okay. Okay. I'll make a phone call to Michael Williams. Find out if what you say is true. Interview suspended nine-fifteen pm."

. . .

"I'm not losing money. My finances are in excellent shape. In fact, I've made a lot of money on the very deals Darryl recommended to me." Michael Williams was adamant.

Yvonne's face paled. "Oh, my God." She left the phone dangling, and ran up to the obs room.

"Dewi, take two uniform officers and get over to Paul Baker's house. Ask Llewellyn for ARV back-up, they should be on standby. Bring him in."

"Will do, ma'am."

"Dewi, surprise will be critical. Don't give him time to arm himself."

"Got you, ma'am."

Tasha took hold of Yvonne's arm. "Are you okay? Things are moving at lightning speed. What's happening?"

"Tasha, we've had the wrong man under surveillance. The killer has been under our radar."

"Paul Baker?"

"Yes, has to be. He gave me a list of clients who were losing money, and one of them was Michael Williams. According to Michael Williams, he's fine. Not lost a penny. In fact he's making."

"You were sold a dud."

"Yes, and there can be only one reason for that."

It was nearly forty minutes later that Dewi called in. "He's not here, ma'am."

"Where is he?"

"We've asked a couple of neighbours, one of them told us they talked to him, as he was leaving the house. He stated he had a late-night meeting."

"Oh no. Come on," Yvonne called to Tasha. "I've got one more question to ask Darryl Williams."

They ran back to the interview room, where Darryl was still seated, looking bemused.

"MR WILLIAMS, which one of your clients is losing money and where does he live?"

"What?"

"Please, I'm sorry, there's no time to waste."

"Er...the only client of ours currently losing out financially is Thomas Childs."

"Thomas Childs, where does he live?"

"He lives near the coastal path in Aberystwyth." He gave them the full address.

Tasha and Yvonne exchanged glances.

Yvonne checked the list of clients for Williams and West, given to her by Baker. "Childs isn't there," she said to Tasha. "He just isn't there."

"It's got to be Paul Baker."

"Let's hope, if he's visiting the Childs family, that we're in time."

"It's ten-twenty pm."

"Let's go."

26

Paul Baker accepted the glass of single malt and relaxed back, on the corner-suite. This had to be one of the biggest study-come-play areas he'd seen. He was relishing being in it, rather than outside in the drizzle, looking in. He stretched his legs out in front of him, circling his feet.

"So, what's with all the secrecy?" Thomas Childs sat opposite, sipping his whisky as though either savouring it or making it last.

"Only a select club know about this deal."

"Is the information good?"

"Very."

"Source?"

"London insider." Baker leaned in towards Childs, maintaining eye contact throughout.

"How come they didn't contact me direct?"

"They asked me to broker it. Muddies the trail to them, if people start asking questions."

Thomas Childs sat back. Something about Baker's eyes

made him uneasy. He'd seen that look before, in West Africa, in a man wild with fever.

"Want another whisky?" Baker eyed the bottle before looking back at Childs.

"Think that'll make it easier to persuade me?" Childs frowned.

"I'm here to help you." Baker lightened his tone. "What have you got to lose? What have you got left to lose."

"That is below the belt."

"Look, I'm guessing it's your house next, right?"

Childs didn't respond.

"Bank looking to repossess this gorgeous place." Baker leaned back, each arm spread outwards, along the top of the corner suite.

"They'll have it over my dead body."

"Exactly."

"What?"

"I mean exactly, that you wouldn't want them to have it. You've worked hard for it. Why give it to them now?"

"I took your advice before and look what that got me."

"What, you mean the oil deal? Look, one deal gone bad doesn't make me a bad adviser. Look at all the times you benefited."

"Boxhall is a big company."

"Of course they are, and it's why you should go for this deal."

"Is this a wild goose chase?" DCI Llewellyn stared at his DI, hands on hips. "I only just sent out the ARV and dogs to Machynlleth."

"I know, sir. Please, can both those teams head up to Aber?"

The DCI sighed. "Where, exactly, am I supposed to send them?"

"I've got the GPS coordinates for you." Yvonne handed him the printed map. "There's more..."?

"Go on."

"I may need a full siege team. Depending on what we find when we get there, we'll need them to hand."

"I thought you said you had to go?"

"I do. I'm gone."

"Keep me up to date. I'll coordinate with the Aber teams from here. I'll come up if I think it necessary. We may need a hostage negotiator."

"You want to be the negotiator?" Yvonne raised both eyebrows.

"Don't be silly." Llewellyn grimaced. "I meant to coordinate in person. So let me know *immediately* what the situation is when you get there."

"I almost forgot, we'll need a warrant for eavesdropping on the house. We'll go straight in if we need to, but our case will be stronger with evidence from his own mouth."

"I'll get a warrant. Keep me informed of every development."

"I will."

"LET'S GO." The DI tapped Tasha on the shoulder and nodded to Dewi. "Program the sat nav, here's the postcode." She handed him her notepad. "There's no time to waste. If he's there, he'll be in full flow. We have to get there in time."

"What if he's not there?" Dewi threw over his shoulder, as they got into their unmarked car.

"I can breathe a sigh of relief, and we begin surveillance with immediate effect."

"Can't we just pick him up?"

"No evidence, Dewi. We have to catch him in the act."

"Of killing?"

"Of asking for the gun as a minimum."

"That's risky." Tasha spoke from the back seat, as the engine purred into life.

"I know." The DI's expression was grave as she turned to face Tasha. "He'll have on him the props he uses to wipe the scene and to leave trace evidence. If he's asked for the gun, and he's got the props in a bag, we should have enough to convict."

"We'll probably get other circumstantial evidence, too." Dewi put his foot down. "Like lack of alibi; setting up deals for the dead families; *and* he may be picked out of a lineup by the rape victims."

"Right, and he may have sandalwood soap in his closet."

"We're going to be relying on your advice if it turns into a siege, Tasha." Yvonne's tone was earnest.

"I'm up for that," Tasha said, her voice firm and even.

27

"That is the end of the bottle." Thomas Childs stood up, his body stiff. His eyes moved to the door and he held his arm out towards it.

Baker frowned "I..."

There was a light tapping on the study door. When it opened, Thomas's wife stood in the doorway, a bath robe over her flimsy nightwear. Baker swallowed hard.

"Sorry to disturb you," she said, blushing, "I just thought I'd let you know I'm off to bed."

Baker's insides churned with thoughts of what he couldn't have.

"I'll be up soon, Marion." Childs gave his wife a warm smile, walking over to rub her on the arm. "Are Christian and Margot asleep?"

"They are. They were asleep before I'd finished the first bedtime story." She smiled, sleepily.

"See you shortly." He placed a light kiss on her forehead.

Baker's insides were as clenched as his fists.

Childs walked back into the middle of the room. "Where were we?"

"I was about to offer you some of this..."
"Ah, Laphroaig..." Childs appeared doubtful.
"Come on, one glass?"
"What the heck, go for it."

ARMED OFFICERS, in full protective gear, alighted from their van, and parked near Baker's Lexus. A stationary vehicle check confirmed it as his.

"He's here. It's his car." Callum shouted down the phone to his DI.

"Here's there, bloody hell, he's there," she cried out loud to Tasha and Dewi. "We've got to save that family!"

"The ARV is on site, still waiting for the dog team." Callum had calmed a little.

It was drizzling again, rendering visibility poor and slowing their journey down perceptibly. Dewi estimated they had a further twenty minutes until they would be at the house. The DI could feel her hands shaking.

"Has anyone got *eyes-on*, Callum?" Yvonne tried to keep the panic out of her voice, but there was still a detectable tremor to it.

"Not yet, ma'am, the blinds are drawn in only one of the downstairs windows, though."

"I'll bet that's where Baker is. Put your ear to the window."

Callum grunted. "I think you mean get the listening equipment out, ma'am?"

"Whatever it takes, Callum. See if you can hear what they're talking about."

"Do we have a warrant?"

"Yes." Yvonne was hoping the DCI had gotten one by now.

"I'll grab ops as soon as they arrive," Callum agreed. "In the meantime, I'll see what I can do myself."

Callum slipped a couple of times on the rain-greased surface, as he found his way around the outside of the large property. He felt a couple of windows, but everything was securely locked. He ducked underneath the windows through which the light poured, listening outside each one. The double-glazing prevented enough noise leakage.

"I can't hear anything, ma'am, not a thing."

"Can you see anything?"

"Not now, no." In the distance, Callum could hear more vehicles arriving. He hoped the DI was one of them and ops another, since he felt pretty useless as the listening device.

He saw torches, and turned his attention back to the house, hoping that Baker and Thomas Childs would not be alerted by them.

"We're on site, Callum. Sit tight. We'll be with you shortly." The DI looked down at her shoes, beyond caring if they would be adequate for the conditions.

Callum only just heard her, his volume was turned so low. He backed away from the property, about to go further down the lane to find her. Childs and Baker had exited the study and were walking through the open-plan kitchen-diner. Callum dropped to the floor, but they didn't look out. He crept towards the window again, trying to ascertain where the men were headed. He couldn't see, from where he was.

"They're on the move through the house, ma'am," he called to Yvonne.

"Both of them?"

"Yes."

"Can you stay eyes-on?"

"Wait. Wait one...Oh my god, they've got a shotgun."

"Who's holding it?"

"Childs, looks like he's carrying it back through to the room with the closed blinds."

Yvonne turned to the ARV and ops team-leaders. "We've got to go in now. They've got the gun."

28

Baker was congratulating himself on turning the situation around. He'd almost lost this one, just like he'd lost the first time he tried it with Ben Davies. Ben's wife had persuaded Ben to go to bed with her. Baker had been afraid tonight was going to go the same way.

He had his hand in Thomas Child's back, guiding him back to the study. Keeping his cool and keeping the banter light. Back in the study, he took the gun from Childs, placing it in his mouth, to the same shocked reaction he'd seen before.

"It's okay," he reassured Childs. "The point is not to pull the trigger, but to feel the gun in your mouth. Feel the fear. Face the menace." His heart-rate had slowed right down. He was ready. "Here." He handed the gun back to Childs. "Your turn."

"I can't." Childs took the gun and made as if to return it back to the gun cupboard.

Baker grabbed his arm. "If you can do this, you can take any risk necessary to get your wealth back." The words were uttered with a calmness aimed at reassuring the man. He was nearly there. "Do it."

Childs turned the gun towards himself and opened his mouth, slowly raising his arms.

OFFICERS HAMMERED the front door with a battering ram. Childs dropped the gun. The colour drained from Baker's face.

"Put the gun away," he hissed at Childs.

"What the hell?" Childs had stepped away from the gun, and was making for the hallway, towards the noise.

"I said put the bloody gun aw-"

Baker was face-to-face with a heavily-armoured police officer, whose gun was aimed directly at him. The colour drained from his face. He raised his hands in surrender and was cuffed from behind.

He was hauled away, just as he heard Marion Childs run to her husband, asking if he was okay. Fear had made her eyes even larger. He turned his head to stop himself from staring.

TASHA PLACED a hand on Yvonne's shoulder. This was a big deal. They had Baker for the family murders. Thomas Childs' testimony, and the stuff they'd found in Baker's bag, would ensure he went away for a considerable time.

They still had to secure enough evidence to convict him for the rapes. The witnesses were brought in one-by-one: Tina Pugh, Sarah Evans and Angela Barnes. They made little conversation with the officers escorting them. The DI acknowledged the women and then returned her eyes to the window. The men walked in. Baker was number three.

The victims knew not to shout out, but Yvonne detected at least two muffled gasps. He hadn't even spoken . She realised at this point that she'd been holding her breath, and she let it out through tight lips. They had him. Not that she'd doubted for one moment. One of the PCs who'd searched him had commented on the sandalwood cologne.

Yvonne thought of her father. She felt as though he'd helped her in this case, even if only through his memory. Helped her save the Childs family and maybe other families whose lives would have been destroyed in the future. Perhaps they would find out why this man did what he did. The psychologists would visit him and decide if he was mad or bad. He'd be imprisoned accordingly. The DI was glad she wouldn't be his probation officer.

29

"When are you due back in London?" Yvonne asked the question, but kept her eyes on the road ahead.

"Last week." Tasha sighed.

"Last week? Really?"

"There's a case waiting for me with the Met, and Kelly is more than a little upset at my still being here."

"Oh." The DI shook her head. "I'm sorry. You should have said. If I'd known, I would never have asked if you wanted to come and meet my sister and her family."

"Hey, I'm my own person, Yvonne. I decide when I go back. I work freelance, remember? The Met can ask, doesn't mean they'll get."

"Yes, but what about Kelly?"

"I know, I do feel guilty about that. But I have Skyped or phoned her most nights, and its only going to be a couple more days now and I'll be home."

Yvonne took her eyes off the road to turn and smile at her friend. "Thanks. It means a lot."

"Besides," Tasha added, "I want to see if they're all as nuts as you."

"You're famous," her sister said, as she hugged her hard.

"I am?"

"You are. You're all over the six o'clock news."

"What are they saying?"

"That you caught a serial killer, and not for the first time."

"She's a superhero." Tasha walked over to Kim, and Yvonne introduced everyone.

"So it's true then." Kim led them inside.

"My *team* caught the killer. I have some amazing people around me. Everyone played their part, including this lady here." She threw the last towards Tasha, who was busy picking up Tom and holding Sally's hand, allowing them to lead her to their favourite toys.

"I realise, now, why you didn't want to tell me what you were working on. That must have been a hard case for you, given what happened to dad, and that Tom and Sally are of similar ages to..." Kim looked across at her children.

"It gave me a few sleepless nights, sis." Yvonne put her arm around her Kim's shoulders. "I came here after some of the worst of them, and you guys made me feel a million times better." Yvonne smiled and grabbed her sister's hands. "Come on, enough of this, let's play."

The DI had one thing left to do before bed. She fired up her sister's laptop, organising her thoughts whilst she waited. She checked the clock – ten pm. She clicked on the Skype icon. It was morning in Adelaide. Her mum was already online.

"Hi, I'm glad you made it." Her mum had her hair tied back. She looked younger.

"Hi, how's things in Adelaide?"

"Good, hot, but not as hot as its gunna get."

"It's cooling down here. Soon be Autumn..."

"Ah yes, that's something I wanted to talk to you about."

"Oh yeah?"

"I'm thinking of visiting the UK at Christmas. How do you feel about that?"

Yvonne paused. After everything that had happened, she felt no anger or irritation at the thought. The woman on the screen was her mother. The woman she had loved absolutely, until the day her father died. She still loved her, and missed her more than she cared to admit.

Yvonne smiled wistfully. "I'd like that. I'd like that a lot. We have so much to talk through, and so much time to catch up on."

"You look tired..." Her mum's eyes creased with concern. "Difficult case?"

"Something like that."

"I can't wait to see you and Kim and to meet Kim's children."

The DI felt a pang of regret, that her mum had never met Tom and Sally. She knew her mother would have come over sooner, had she thought her eldest daughter amenable. Not being able to talk to Yvonne had made it too painful to return to the UK.

"Are you bringing *him*?"

"That depends on you."

"Do you want to?"

"I'd like to, but not if it makes things difficult."

"It'll be fine." Yvonne's shoulders relaxed. What harm could it do, now?

"We'll book a hotel for around two weeks-"

"Please," Yvonne's face was earnest, "stay at mine. It's big enough, and Kim and the children can stay, too."

Her mother appeared to seriously consider, pausing for several seconds, then: "That's a lovely offer, Yvonne, perhaps in the future? But, I think this first time, a hotel might be best."

Yvonne nodded. "Okay, well, if you change your mind..."

"I'll know where to come."

As Yvonne closed down the laptop, Tasha gently tapped the door.

"Come on in," the DI called, still seated cross-legged on the bed.

"Did you do it?" Tasha sat herself on the corner.

"I did." Yvonne sighed. "I don't really know why it's taken me so long."

"One word, grief."

"It's not even about what she said, but what she didn't say, back then. Like, because we were children, that we'd recover okay. That we wouldn't need so much time. That our friends and school and our social lives would make the sadness go that much quicker. Our feelings weren't given the same importance."

"Your mum was grieving, too, and probably feeling hugely guilty. She may have been thinking all sorts of things, she just didn't know how to convey them to you. She would probably have been worried about your reaction."

"Yes, you could be right."

"You probably went through something similar when

David died, with certain of your friends and acquaintances. The people whose heads went down, as they crossed the street, or those you just didn't see for a while, because they were avoiding you. Some people find it hard to say the right words. So they don't say them. They don't say anything at all."

"She was our mother."

"Mothers are many things, Yvonne. Very few of them are perfect. Just like the rest of us."

"You're going to tell me next, I'd understand better if I was one." Yvonne smiled, she understood exactly what Tasha meant.

"Maybe," Tasha grinned sheepishly. "I wouldn't know, either."

"Thank you, Tasha. Thank you for everything over the last few weeks."

"You're welcome. Though, you know, if we carry on like this I'm going to have to move to Wales. It'd be far easier than having to up sticks every few months." The psychologist winked at her.

"Don't joke. As well as being the best friend ever, you're a fantastic resource for our squad."

"Kelly wouldn't be happy. Her life is in London."

"Oh yes." Yvonne looked down. "Of course, I forgot."

"Hey, come on...I have some news for you."

"You do?"

"Remember Mark Grantham?"

"How could I forget."

"I came in to tell you about a call I just had from a friend. Turns out Mr Grantham's being investigated by the fraud office. He has a lot of questions to answer."

"What about Ryan Smith?"

"He's not being investigated currently, but if he's still

linked – as we believe he is – to Boxhall, and they're working in cahoots, I think this time fraud will nail them."

"We'll see. Money talks."

PAUL BAKER PACED HIS CELL. He could hear noise from the other inmates, shouting to each other and occasionally banging their doors or walls. He heard what he thought was stuff being hauled up through windows, on makeshift ropes. He'd washed the toilet umpteen times with the soap from his basin. It still stank, to the point he almost couldn't bear it.

He glanced around: bed, toilet, small cupboard, and wash basin. It wasn't much to show for his life. Still, as a serial killer and sex-offender, at least he was guaranteed his own cell, for now. Small things mattered big, in this place.

He thought of the DI. He'd be in here a few years, until he could figure a way out. But, after that? That trumped-up little bitch better keep looking over her shoulder. And when he finished? There were still a few countries a fugitive could hide out. Especially if they had money.

∽

THE END

AFTERWORD

If you enjoyed this book, I'd be very grateful if you'd post a short review on Amazon. Your support really does make a difference and helps bring my books to more readers like you.

Mailing list: You can join my emailing list here : AnnamarieMorgan.com
Facebook page: AnnamarieMorganAuthor

You might also like to read the other books in the series:
Book 1: Death Master:
After months of mental and physical therapy, Yvonne Giles, an Oxford DI, is back at work and that's just how she likes it. So when she's asked to hunt the serial killer responsible for taking apart young women, the DI jumps at the chance but hides the fact she is suffering debilitating flashbacks. She is told to work with Tasha Phillips, an in-her-face, criminal psychologist. The DI is not enamoured with the idea. Tasha has a lot to prove. Yvonne has a lot to get over. A tentative link with a 20 year-old cold case brings

them closer to the truth but events then take a horrifyingly personal turn.

Book 2: You Will Die

After apprehending an Oxford Serial Killer, and almost losing her life in the process, DI Yvonne Giles has left England for a quieter life in rural Wales. Her peace is shattered when she is asked to hunt a priest-killing psychopath, who taunts the police with messages inscribed on the corpses. Yvonne requests the help of Dr. Tasha Phillips, a psychologist and friend, to aid in the hunt. But the killer is one step ahead and the ultimatum, he sets them, could leave everyone devastated.

Book 3: Total Wipeout

A whole family is wiped out with a shotgun. At first glance, it's an open-and-shut case. The dad did it, then killed himself. The deaths follow at least two similar family wipeouts – attributed to the financial crash.

So why doesn't that sit right with Detective Inspector Yvonne Giles? And why has a rape occurred in the area, in the weeks preceding each family's demise? Her seniors do not believe there are questions to answer. DI Giles must therefore risk everything, in a high-stakes investigation of a mysterious masonic ring and players in high finance.

Can she find the answers, before the next innocent family is wiped out?

Book 4: Deep Cut

In a tiny hamlet in North Wales, a female recruit is murdered whilst on Christmas home leave. Detective Inspector Yvonne Giles is asked to cut short her own leave, to investigate. Why was the young soldier killed? And is her death related to several alleged suicides at her army base? DI Giles this it is, and that someone powerful has a dark secret they will do anything to hide.

Book 5: The Pusher

Young men are turning up dead on the banks of the River Severn. Some of them have been missing for days or even weeks. The only thing the police can be sure of, is that the men have drowned. Rumours abound that a mythical serial killer has turned his attention from the Manchester canal to the waterways of Mid-Wales. And now one of CID's own is missing. A brand new recruit with everything to live for. DI Giles must find him before it's too late.

Book 6: Gone

Children are going missing. They are not heard from again until sinister requests for cryptocurrency go viral. The public must pay or the children die. For lead detective Yvonne Giles, the case is complicated enough. And then the unthinkable happens...

Book 7: Bone Dancer

A serial killer is murdering women, threading their bones back together, and leaving them for police to find. Detective Inspector Yvonne Giles must find him before more innocent victims die. Problem is, the killer wants her and will do anything he can to get her. Unaware that she, herself, is is a target, DI Giles risks everything to catch him.

Book 8: Blood Lost

A young man comes home to find his whole family missing. Half-eaten breakfasts and blood spatter on the lounge wall are the only clues to what happened...

Book 9: Angel of Death

He is watching. Biding his time. Preparing himself for a torturous kill. Soaring above; lord of all. His journey, direct through the lives of the unsuspecting.

The Angel of Death is nigh.

The peace of the Mid-Wales countryside is shattered, when a female eco-warrior is found crucified in a public wood. At first, it would appear a simple case of finding which of the woman's enemies had had her killed. But DI Yvonne Giles has no idea how bad things are going to get. As the body count rises, she will need all of her instincts, and the skills of those closest to her, to stop the murderous rampage of the Angel of Death.

Book 10: Death in the Air

Several fatal air collisions have occurred within a few months in rural Wales. According to the local Air Accidents Investigation Branch (AAIB) inspector, it's a coincidence. Clusters happen. Except, this cluster is different. DI Yvonne Giles suspects it when she hears some of the witness statements but, when an AAIB inspector is found dead under a bridge, she knows it.

Something is way off. Yvonne is determined to get to the bottom of the mystery, but exactly how far down the treacherous rabbit hole is she prepared to go?

Book 11: Death in the Mist

The morning after a viscous sea-mist covers the seaside town of Aberystwyth, a young student lies brutalised within one hundred yards of the castle ruins.

DI Yvonne Giles' reputation precedes her. Having successfully captured more serial killers than some detectives have caught colds, she is seconded to head the murder investigation team, and hunt down the young woman's killer.

What she doesn't know, is this is only the beginning...

Book 12: Death under Hypnosis

When the secretive and mysterious Sheila Winters approaches Yvonne Giles and tells her that she murdered someone thirty years before, she has the DI's immediate attention.

Things get even more strange when Sheila states:

She doesn't know who.

She doesn't know where.

She doesn't know why.

Book 13: Fatal Turn

A seasoned hiker goes missing from the Dolfor Moors after recording a social media video describing a narrow cave he intends to explore. A tragic accident? Nothing to see here, until a team of cavers disappear on a coastal potholing expedition, setting off a string of events that has DI Giles tearing her hair out. What, or who is the thread that ties this series of disappearances together?

A serial killer, thriller murder-mystery set in Wales.

Book 14: The Edinburgh Murders

A newly retired detective from the Met is murdered in a murky alley in Edinburgh, a sinister calling card left with the body.

The dead man had been a close friend of psychologist Tasha Phillips, giving her her first gig with the Met decades before.

Tasha begs DI Yvonne Giles to aid the Scottish police in solving the case.

In unfamiliar territory, and with a ruthless killer haunting the streets, the DI plunges herself into one of the darkest, most terrifying cases of her career. Who exactly is The Poet?

Remember to watch out for Book 15, coming soon...

Printed in Great Britain
by Amazon